Cambodian Folk Stories from the *Gatiloke*

Cambodian Folk Stories from the *Gatiloke*

retold by Muriel Paskin Carrison
from a translation by The Venerable Kong Chhean

TUTTLE PUBLISHING
Boston • Rutland, Vermont • Tokyo

Published by Tuttle Publishing
an imprint of Periplus Editions (HK) Ltd.

LCC Card No. 86-51325
ISBN 0-8048-1905-X

First paperback edition, 1993
Third printing, 2002

Printed in Singapore

Distributed by:

Japan & Korea
Tuttle Publishing
RK Building 2nd Floor
2-13-10 Shimo-Meguro, Meguro-ku
Tokyo 153 0064
Tel: (03) 5437 0171
Fax: (03) 5437 0755

North America
Tuttle Publishing
Distribution Center
Airport Industrial Park
364 Innovation Drive
North Clarendon, VT 05759-9436
Tel: (802) 773 8930
Fax: (802) 773 6993

Asia Pacific
Berkeley Books Pte. Ltd.
130 Joo Seng Road
#06-01/03 Olivine Building
Singapore 368357
Tel: (65) 280 1330
Fax: (65) 280 6290

To my mother and father
Hattie and Jacob Paskin
who taught me to value the common humanity in all people
and to cherish the gift of their differences

Note: The spelling of Cambodian words in the Roman alphabet is often very complicated, and no one system of romanization is accepted by everyone. We have simplified the spelling of several Cambodian words and names.

TABLE OF CONTENTS

MAP
Cambodia and Neighboring Countries   108, 109

ACKNOWLEDGMENTS

I am grateful to the many people who have helped me in the preparation of this book. I wish to thank them.

Dr. Franklin E. Huffman, professor of linguistics and Asian studies, Cornell University, and author of the *English-Khmer Dictionary*, graciously sent me a duplicate of his rare copy of the ten-volume original *Gatiloke*. These Khmer volumes have made it possible for Dr. Kong and me to prepare this book for English readers.

Dr. Dan Ben-Amos, professor and chairman, Department of Folklore and Folklife, University of Pennsylvania, understood my wish to reach a wide audience of school-age children and lay adults in order to further the appreciation of Cambodian culture by the English-speaking public. His approval of my goals and encouragement of my work have meant a great deal to me.

In approaching this work, I often became discouraged not only by my own limitations, but also with the limited availability of materials on Cambodian history and culture. I am deeply grateful to Dr. Philip N. Jenner, professor of Cambodian and Southeast Asian literatures, University of Hawaii, for being my constant mentor during the past four years. He was attentive to my needs and generous in sharing his personal materials on Cambodian life and culture. Dr. Jenner also shared with me his empathetic understanding of the Cambodian people and the plight of the refugees.

I would also like to thank the Venerable Kong Chhean, who always found time to help me. He carefully guided my understanding of Theravada Buddhism and skillfully instructed me on the finer points of Cambodian life.

The members of the Cambodian community of Southern California were most helpful in supplying me with needed books, illustrations, and photographs. I am grateful to them for graciously inviting me to their community festivals and to their private celebrations.

My sons, Michael Lombrozo and Peter Lombrozo gave me their expert help in the preparation of illustrative materials for this volume. The illustrations on pages 2, 24, 28, 33, 48, 75, 88, and 125 are based on drawings by Paul E. Smythe. The maps on page 108 are based on the work of Jason Edward Berri. Some of the other illustrative material has been adapted from *Geography, First Level*, and *Cambodian Reading, Grade Two*, Cambodian elementary-school textbooks printed by UNESCO and found in the library collection of the Asian Cultural Centre for UNESCO, Tokyo, Japan.

Finally, I wish to thank my "volunteer" proofreaders— my aunt Ruth Ganeles and my friends Annetta Moore and Katherine Berry.

—Muriel Paskin Carrison

Huntington Beach, California

INTRODUCTION

The Gatiloke (GAH-tee-Low-kah) is a collection of folk stories that is part of the very ancient literary tradition of Cambodia. For hundreds—even thousands—of years, these stories were told from generation to generation by word of mouth. It was only in the late nineteenth century that they were written down and published. The stories in our book have been translated from this written collection.

FOLK STORIES

For thousands of years, people all over the world have loved to listen to stories. Some stories explained why the stars twinkle or the ocean roars; some stories were magical fancies about superhuman men who could lift the earth or walk on water; some stories were jokes and riddles for laughter and entertainment; and some stories were very important lessons for living successfully and happily with family and friends.

Because stories have always been such a treasured part

of people's lives, they have often been called "folktales" or "folklore." "Folk" means "the people." "Tale" is from an old Danish word meaning "speech," and "lore" is from an old German word which meant "to teach." Before writing systems were invented, the only way people could pass on their histories, customs, and beliefs from generation to generation was by telling stories. This telling and retelling of stories could almost be called a "speech-teach."

The folktales of the Gatiloke were used by Cambodian Buddhist monks as "speech-teach" sermons—examples of right and wrong, good and bad. The word "Gatiloke" reflects this: *Gati* means "the way," and *loke* means "the world." Freely translated, "Gatiloke" means "the right way for the people of the world to live."

THE BUDDHA

These ideas about the right and wrong way to live came from the teachings of Gautama Siddhartha, who was a prince in India in about 500 B.C. In India, there was a system of castes, or strict social classes. The Brahmans were the highest caste. They were priests and controlled the Hindu religious practices of the country. Prince Gautama was a member of the second caste, the Kshatriyas, or rulers. He was disturbed by the suffering of the people caused by the injustices that had developed within the Hindu religion in India. He left his family and wealth to think about how people could live better and happier lives. After many years of wandering and meditating, he found the "right way"—he became "enlightened." From then on he was called the Buddha, the Enlightened One. His followers were called Buddhists and his philosophy called Buddhism.

In many ways, Buddhism was a social protest movement against the Hindu caste system with its superstitious obedience to the Brahmans and its bloody sacrifices of humans and animals. In his sermons about the right way to live, Buddha refuted the caste system, claiming that all people were equal and that governments should be democratic and just. Buddha preached that there are no superhuman gods or kings, that man is his own master, and that no higher deity sits in judgment over his destiny. He spoke out against human and animal sacrifices, superstition, and belief in magical ceremonies. Everyone was responsible to think for himself, using reason and logic to make wise and compassionate judgments. His teachings to his followers are summed up in the Eightfold Path—eight rules that advise people to try to have good beliefs, speech, actions, work, efforts, mindfulness, strength of purpose, and self-understanding.

Almost all religions are built upon some kind of faith— often a "blind" faith. But in Buddhism, the emphasis is upon individual self-reliance: observing, knowing, understanding, and doing. In this way, Buddhism is different from most Western religions in that there is no belief in gods or saints, heaven or hell. Buddhism is more like an ethical philosophy of life—a right way for the people to live together peacefully and to act with wisdom and compassion.

FOLK STORIES OF THE BUDDHIST MONKS

After the death of the Buddha, his followers (monks) began traveling to distant places to spread his teachings. Eventually, Buddhism split into two large branches. One, the Theravada branch, was brought to Cambodia and other parts of Southeast Asia. The other, the Mahayana branch, spread to China, Japan, and other countries.

From the very beginning, the Buddhist monks were not content with just talking about the wise words of the Enlightened One; they also tried to reach the people by teaching and explaining. They always seemed to have a keen delight in telling stories to illustrate their sermons. They composed many new stories, and they also collected old legends, anecdotes, and jokes which they remodeled in the spirit of Buddhism.

Some of these Buddhist stories are rooted in ancient Stone Age beliefs in spirits and magic. Some were probably originally carried from western Asia by tribes that began migrating about five thousand years ago into both Europe and India. From India, stories were carried by merchants and by Buddhist missionaries into Southeast Asia, China, and Japan. This is one reason for the appearance of many stories, such as the Cinderella legend and the Tar Baby story, in the folklore of countries as far apart as Ireland and Indonesia. Although many of the Buddhist monks' stories must have existed in some form in Asia for centuries before the rise of Buddhism, the monks gave the tales a style and flavor all their own.

In traditional Western folk stories, the hero or heroine is usually a beautiful and good person who after much suffering is finally rewarded with great wealth and perfect happiness. The ancient Asian stories so loved by the Buddhist monks were not concerned with larger-than-life heroes and heroines and their grand rewards. Because the heart and mind of Buddhism rested with common folk and their daily lives, the monks chose the folk stories about ordinary daily events to teach the people the "right way" to live. The monks' stories are not tales of superhuman feats, but are concerned with the virtues of prudence, moderation, and foresight. The tales are not about a world filled with make-believe, but about the problems of artisans, merchants, farmers, and slaves— the people about whom the Brahmans had so little to say.

Here is what the monks said about certain subjects:

Human relations: Theravada Buddhists believed that all men and women were equal. Therefore, many stories poke fun at the foolishness, greed, and stupidity of kings, lords, high government officials, and even the gods—often the old Hindu gods.

Individual responsibility: The Buddhist point of view was that each person was responsible for his own actions. There were no excuses for foolishness or ignorance. All people had an obligation to think wisely and to use reason before acting. Buddhism was not sympathetic to people who became the victims of scoundrels, rascals, or con artists. In many stories, the victim rightfully suffered because he neglected to think wisely or because he stupidly believed in magic.

Punishment and reward: Buddhists were not so much concerned with the immediate punishment of the villain. They believed that his spirit would be reborn in a different body (reincarnation). Then, he would suffer many hardships in his new life because of the bad deeds of his present life. Often the monks' stories end with the culprit free and happy, living with his stolen goods, while the victim suffers.

Likewise, a person who does good deeds—"acts of merit," as they are called—is reborn into a better life. Eventually, after more rebirths, such a person has a perfect soul. This is called "nirvana." When this perfect state is reached, the individual remains like that forever and no longer has to be reborn.

Killing animals: From the time of their opposition to the Brahman practices of human and animal sacrifices, Buddhists have always preached against killing. In many stories, cruel and insensitive hunters are outwitted by kind and intelligent animals. In other stories, animals are depicted as far wiser than the human beings or gods who live near them.

Greed and ingratitude: The Buddhist monks always tried to remind the people to live their lives with kindness and compassion. Stories were told about people who became victims of their own greed and ingratitude.

CAMBODIAN BUDDHIST FOLK STORIES

When traveling missionaries brought Buddhism to Cambodia more than two thousand years ago, Cambodia already had a highly developed civilization. For example, the people of Cambodia and of other Southeast Asian countries had always held women in high esteem. These people embraced the teachings of Buddha that the missionaries brought, but rejected the traditional Indian treatment of women as mere "possessions" to serve the wishes and needs of their husbands and lords. Some of the Cambodian Buddhist stories teach respect for women, telling about their intelligent virtues and of the unfortunate things that happened to men who did not treat women justly as equals.

Over the centuries, the Buddhist stories brought by the missionaries merged with the folklore already in Cambodia to create a unique body of literature in the spirit of Buddhism and Cambodian life. The collection of folk-tales known as the Gatiloke is part of this mixture of Buddhist and native Cambodian stories.

The setting of the Gatiloke stories is usually a town, village, or forest where the ordinary people live and work. They have the usual strengths and weaknesses of people all over the world. Problems occur as they go about the business of daily living.

The monks' stories of the Gatiloke were gentle warnings to all the people to follow the "right way." The Gatiloke has charming stories of clever women who foil traps set for them by nobles and of peasants whose quick wit saves them from thieves and scoundrels. Animal fables have lessons in wisdom, justice, and compassion. Humorous tales ridicule unjust rulers or tell of the absurd predica-ments of foolish people. Many stories deplore the short-comings of kings, generals, and their ministers. Other stories warn Buddhists to stay away from the stuff of the Brahmans: greed for riches, belief in magical ceremonies, and the practices of human or animal sacrifices.

The folk story is an important part of the cultural his-tory of a people. Although the folktales of the world share the dreams and predicaments common to all people, in each culture there are ideas not found in other cultures. The Gatiloke stories are a rich body of oral literature which tells about the daily life, problems, and humor of the Cambodian people—the unique spirit of the nation. Each story has its own points of interest and beauty.

Just as Buddhism became one of the great religions of the world, the Cambodian Buddhist literature belongs to the literary heritage of the world and should be made the common property of all peoples. A traditional defense of the classics is that they shed light on human problems that do not change from generation to generation. We are all the fortunate heirs to the treasure-house of the classical Cambodian literature.

The stories in this book have been selected from the 112 Gatiloke stories written down in the late nineteenth century by Oknha Sotann Preychea Ind, a Buddhist monk who was commissioned by the Cambodian government to collect popular folktales for preservation and publication. The monk's work is the first and only known written collection of the Gatiloke stories in the Cambodian language, and as far as we know, our book contains the first English translation of stories from this collection.

As political refugees, many Cambodians have recently emigrated to the United States and other nations. They bring with them an ancient heritage rich in art, music, and literature about which the West knows so very little. It therefore gives us great pleasure to present this selection of stories. We hope that they will bring delight, enjoyment, and understanding of the Cambodian people to the English-speaking peoples of the world.

PREFACE and EPILOGUE
to the "Gatiloke"

(late nineteenth century)

My name is Oknha Sotann Preychea Ind. I wrote and composed this *Gatiloke* for young children who are interested in studying tradition and morality, and in comparing these traditions to the more modern world which exists today.

I also composed questions and answers so that it would be easier for the children to understand. . . . For example, if the student asks the teacher, "Venerable, what does the word 'Gatiloke' mean?" the teacher may answer, " 'Gatiloke' means all the things that are going on in the world. . . . *Loke* means 'the world,' and . . . *gati* should mean 'the path,' 'the way of morality.' "

* * *

I composed this *Gatiloke* from collected short stories. If I have made any mistakes, please forgive me. Please ask a more intelligent and better scholar to correct my mistakes.

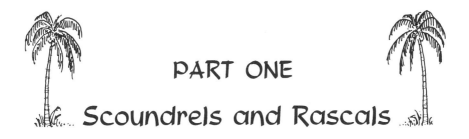

PART ONE
Scoundrels and Rascals

The Story of Princess Amaradevi

In a small kingdom of Kampuchea, there once lived a wealthy princess by the name of Amaradevi who was an educated and talented young woman. Now, there were four old grand ministers of the palace who unfortunately had no appreciation of Amaradevi's many accomplishments, but, being attracted by her riches, they all wished to marry her. Princess Amaradevi kindly rejected their proposals, choosing instead to marry a fine young man whose name was Mahoseth Pandide.

Amaradevi and Mahoseth loved and respected each other. They lived happily together in peace and harmony. But the four grand ministers were very bitter and resentful. Whenever they spoke to Mahoseth, they tried to be as insulting and offensive as possible. They even started vicious rumors throughout the palace, claiming that Mahoseth Pandide was disloyal to the king. Then they began to whisper to the king himself that Mahoseth was dishonest and deceitful. The gentle king, who loved his daughter and her husband, urged the ministers to be more reasonable and cautious in their accusations. But the more the king urged, the more determined the ministers became to destroy Mahoseth.

One day, they decided to tell the king that Mahoseth Pandide was plotting to kill him and take the throne. This time, their arguments and false proofs were so convincing that the king believed them. Without even giving Mahoseth Pandide a chance to defend himself, the angry king ordered him to leave the country immediately and never return.

The four ruthless ministers were satisfied with the

result of their schemes. Delighted with their success, they congratulated each other and began plotting their next steps. "Of course," First Grand Minister Senak advised, "we do not know which one of us Amaradevi will wish to marry. We must each ask her, one at a time. Then after she chooses and marries one of us, we will divide her riches equally. But now, she must be mourning for her foolish husband. So let us wait two weeks from today before we talk with her."

Meanwhile, with her husband banished from the kingdom forever, Amaradevi passed the days in sorrow. She blamed herself for not being able to save her husband. She had known that the powerful grand ministers had wanted to marry her for her money. She had known that the ministers had plotted against her beloved husband. So each day as she paced back and forth in her palace rooms, she relived her own stupidity and tried to think of a way to prove to the king that Mahoseth had always been loyal and that the four ministers had been the real evil plotters.

"Oh, you greedy, wretched monsters!" she would cry to herself. "I will find a way to punish you. I will never be your rich puppet-wife. I will find a way to have my Mahoseth returned to me. I will find a way to teach you to respect and honor a woman's mind and heart."

Two weeks after Mahoseth Pandide's banishment, First Grand Minister Senak came to visit Amaradevi with his proposals of love and marriage. Amaradevi listened to him quietly and slowly replied, "Yes, my dear Senak, I am quite lonesome. Perhaps I could love you and marry you. If you wish to visit with me, why not return later this evening, at seven o'clock?"

First Grand Minister Senak was delighted. He bowed excessively and promised to return at the appointed time.

During the same morning, Amaradevi was surprised by the visits of the other three ministers. It seemed that almost as soon as one left, another appeared. They all praised her beauty, professed their love, and begged her to marry them. Amaradevi was polite to all of them. As they left, she graciously invited each one to visit with her that same evening. The second grand minister, Pakkos, she told to come at eight o'clock. The third grand minister, Kapindu, she told to come at nine o'clock. And the fourth grand minister, Devin, she told to come at ten. But all that morning, as Amaradevi had been listening quietly to the four unscrupulous ministers, she had been trying to think of a way to entrap them and prove their treachery to the king. Now, Amaradevi had been educated not only in music, painting, and the fine art of poetry but also in government, law, the sciences, and engineering construction. Being so talented, she was quite capable of planning a clever strategy that would ensnare the falsehearted ministers and at the same time legally prove their villainy to the king.

Soon after the last grand minister left, Amaradevi summoned her servants to her palace rooms. First she instructed them on how to dig a huge pit under the floor of her small back parlor, and how to prevent it from caving in. Next, she told them how to make a special mixture of mud, hot water, and sticky rice in a large caldron. The servants then poured this mixture into the pit, filling it halfway. Finally, Amaradevi skillfully taught the servants how to construct a trap door to cover the large hole. The trap door was operated by a rope secretly hidden behind a curtained recess.

When the construction work was finished, Amaradevi dismissed the servants and sent for her personal maid. She ordered her maid to bring all of her precious jewels and pile them carelessly on a table near the trap door in the small back parlor. When that was done, Amaradevi told the maid to expect the visits of the four grand ministers. The maid was to welcome them respectfully and ask them politely to wait for the princess in the small back parlor. The maid bowed obediently, and Amaradevi continued, "When each man arrives and is in the small back parlor, please come to me."

That evening, promptly at seven o'clock, first Grand Minister Senak arrived. The maid graciously greeted him and led him to the small back parlor. Then she walked softly to her mistress's rooms. Amaradevi rose quickly, saying to the maid, "Follow me quietly and do as I tell you."

The maid followed after Amaradevi to the small back parlor. They slipped silently behind the curtained recess, waited, and watched. First Grand Minister Senak was bending over the table of glistening jewels. He put his hand out to touch one. Then he quickly pulled his hand back to his side and stepped back. He paced the room a bit and slowly returned to the table, putting his hand out once more, then down again. The jewels were like magnets, pulling his hands to them. He just must touch one. He looked around the room and through the doorway. Then, quickly reaching out, he grabbed a huge ruby and stuffed it deep into his pocket. At that moment, Amaradevi signaled her maid. Both women pulled hard on the rope. The trap door opened, throwing First Grand Minister Senak screaming into the large pit of warm mud and sticky rice. Then the heavy trap door closed neatly and tightly, muffling the wretched man's shouts.

The three other grand ministers arrived at their appointed times. Each in turn was politely greeted by the maid. Each in turn was asked to wait for the princess in the small back parlor. And each in turn became bewitched by the table of shimmering rubies, emeralds, and diamonds. None of them could resist the temptation of

stuffing at least one of the jewels into his pocket. As each grand minister stuffed his pocket, the two women pulled the trap-door rope, throwing another wretched man into the deep pit filled with warm mud and sticky rice. As each grand minister fell into the pit, the mud and sticky rice rose higher and higher until the men could barely breathe. As they thrashed about trying to escape, they almost choked on the drying mud and swelling rice.

Amaradevi kept the trap door tightly closed all night. The next morning, she told her servants to take the mud-caked ministers out of the pit, bind their hands, and lead them to the royal court. In solemn dignity, she followed behind them. When they reached the throne room, the princess bowed before her father. With great restraint, she spoke. "Your Majesty, I ask your permission to prove to the royal court the perfidy of these four grand ministers of the palace."

The king nodded, and Amaradevi continued. "The grand ministers all asked for my hand in marriage because they were greedy for my riches. When I refused their proposals and married the good Mahoseth Pandide, they plotted against him, finally convincing the royal court that he was disloyal and dishonest. Now the ministers have come to me again with proposals of love and marriage. But the only thing that they really love is our royal jewels. I trapped them as they were stealing our sacred treasures from my apartments. I will prove this to you. Now you will know who the guilty traitors really are."

Amaradevi signaled her maid. The woman reached

into each grand minister's pocket, pulled out a precious royal jewel, and held it up before everyone's eyes.

The king was both saddened and furious. He ordered the palace guards to tie the mud-caked ministers to elephants and drag them through the streets for all the people to see.

Amaradevi bowed to the king and returned to her palace rooms.

The word "Kampuchea" is a Cambodian name for the country. It is derived from "Kambuja," the name of the legendary father of the Cambodian people.

Toward the end of the thirteenth century, Chou Ta-kuan, a Chinese traveler who visited Cambodia, was surprised to find that the women of the country were so highly respected and that they held many important political posts at court. His report to the emperor of China also praised the women's knowledge of astrology and government affairs. Chou Ta-kuan wrote that one woman was so greatly talented and educated that she composed her husband's entire biography in beautiful metered Sanskrit verse.

At a time when most of the world treated women as lowly possessions, Cambodians had ancient traditions of respecting their women as important human beings and treating them as equals. These traditional relationships became strained at certain times when Cambodian kings adopted the Brahman customs of treating women as inferior to men. Cambodian monks told this tale to remind the people that women were as intelligent and capable as men and that they should be treated with human dignity.

The Tbal Kdoong

Once there was a rich young widow who lived in the countryside with her brothers and sisters. Their house was quite isolated from the village. But the widow was grateful to be with her relatives because her baby was frail and sickly.

Now, a scoundrel living in the village knew that this widow was rich. Each time he passed the lonely country-side house, he thought of her riches and planned ways to rob her. Soon the summer came and the young widow's brothers and sisters left for the rice fields each morning. The widow remained home alone with her sickly baby.

When the scoundrel learned that the widow was alone, he shaved his head and stole a saffron-yellow robe from the monastery. Then he dressed himself like a Buddhist monk and walked down the country road to the widow's secluded house. When he reached the front of the house, he stopped and stood quietly. The young widow was sitting there with her baby. She saw the yellow-robed man standing patiently, and thought he was a Buddhist monk. In reverence, she carried her baby to him and said, "Venerable Sir, from which temple do you come? What do you wish?"

The scoundrel spoke to her imitating the mannered speech of monks. "Madam, I hark from the temple yonder to gather incense and candles for my meditation ceremony. Dear madam, how many people abide with you and where may they now be?"

The widow answered, "Venerable Sir, my seven brothers and sisters live with me, but they left for the rice fields early this morning."

"Dear madam, why did you not go with them?"

The widow replied, "Reverend, I did not go with them because my baby is always sick. He cries all day, all the time."

And the scoundrel questioned her again: "Madam, what kind of sickness does your baby have?"

The widow answered, "Venerable Sir, I do not know, but sometimes my baby feels very cold. Then sometimes he feels very hot. He cries so much that sometimes I think he will die."

The scoundrel sighed, "Oh, poor baby! I love this baby very much! How I love this beautiful baby! Why have you not taken him to the doctor?"

"Reverend Sir, I took my baby to many doctors, but none of them could cure him."

Then the imposter boasted, "Ah! I know all about this disease. I used to cure such diseases a long time ago and I can do so again. Do not worry anymore."

The young widow begged, "O Reverend Sir, do help us, for I am alone and I have no husband."

Then the scoundrel told the widow to prepare a *slathorby-say* altar with incense, candles, and bananas. When the widow had arranged everything, she invited the scoundrel to sit inside her house and she quietly paid reverence to him near the ceremonial prayer altar.

After a while, the scoundrel asked her if she had a mill for grinding rice—a *tbal kdoong*—nearby.

"Yes, Reverend Sir. There is one behind the house."

Then the scoundrel said, "I suggest that you take your baby to the *tbal kdoong* and set him in the large bowl under

SLATHORBYSAY ALTAR

the grinder. I tell you to do this because a ghost is always with your baby filling him with a great sickness. When you set your baby under the grinder of the *tbal kdoong,* the ghost will be afraid of being smashed and will run away."

The widow obeyed and took her baby to the *tbal kdoong* and set him in the large bowl under the grinder.

"Now," said the scoundrel, "jump up on the lever."

Again the widow obeyed. She got up onto the lever. When the lever went down, the grinder rose up.

"Good," the scoundrel nodded. "Stay like that for a little while. I will go into the house and bring the incense and candles outside here for our prayer ceremony."

And so the scoundrel went into the house and stole the

TBAL KDOONG

young widow's jewels and diamonds and money. Then he ran away.

The widow could not do anything. She could not run after the scoundrel because if she jumped off the lever of the *tbal kdoong,* the grinder would come down and her baby would be crushed. It was no use calling for help because no one was at home and there were no neighbors nearby. So she stood on the lever of the *tbal kdoong* for the whole day, and the scoundrel ran safely away with her riches.

Just as most people did thousands of years ago, the ancient peoples of Southeast Asia worshiped the spirits of animals, trees, and stones, and they believed in the powers of magic. Throughout the centuries, these beliefs were passed on from generation to generation. Even when the Cambodian people embraced the more sophisticated philosophies of Buddhism, many of them still continued to believe in their ancient magic rituals. Theravada Buddhist monks were always trying to free the people from their dependence on such superstition. In this "modern" story, the unfortunate young woman suffered because, instead of reasoning wisely, she stupidly believed in magical ceremonies.

The Story of
Tah Tyen and Chow Saun

Once there was a Buddhist novice who was called Tah Tyen because he was so lazy that he hardly worked at all. He spent most of his time wandering through the village begging alms for food and drink, and spent very little of his time at the monastery studying or working.

One day, this shiftless novice met up with three other lazy rascals of the village. They decided that since they were too lazy to work, they would steal farmers' chickens for their dinners and use Tah Tyen's alms money to buy their *sraa*. Now, the good villagers soon lost patience with these pranks, and the monks would no longer tolerate Tah Tyen's disgraceful behavior. (Buddhist monks are forbidden to kill animals, to steal, to drink wine, or to eat after midday.) So the monks expelled Tah Tyen from the monastery, and the villagers refused to give him any more alms. Tah Tyen and his three friends were upset when they had no more money to buy *sraa* and nothing to eat.

"Look," Tah Tyen proposed to his friends, "we cannot stay here any longer. The people hide their chickens from you and they turn their heads away from me when I ask for alms. They do not trust us here anymore. We must move on to another village—one where the people do not know us. Besides, I've decided that I don't like the life of a meditation monk anyway. So let's prepare our umbrellas and our mosquito nets, steal some food and a few monks' robes, and leave. If I wear my monk's robe and the three of you walk behind me as if you are my novice disciples, then the people in the next village will give us a lot of alms. Then we can buy *sraa* and get drunk again."

The three rascals agreed with Tah Tyen. They gathered their belongings and left the village. That night they slept in the forest near a village in the next district. Early the following morning, Tah Tyen, dressed in his saffron-yellow monk's robe, took up his alms bowl and, with his three friends walking respectfully behind him, pro-

ALM'S BOWL

ceeded into the village. As they approached the crowded village square, the three men called out, "Oh, our teacher is truly the world's wonder! He knows how to tell fortunes. He knows much magic that will cure all sickness. He asks nothing for himself. He only wants to help you. We are his faithful and devoted followers because we have seen his miracles."

All the people in the square who heard the three men believed them. The simple villagers felt very honored to have Tah Tyen in their town. They willingly filled his alms bowl with many *riel* and *kahk* coins. In return, Tah Tyen chanted some prayers that he had memorized and performed a few magic tricks that he had learned.

In a short while, the scoundrels found their arms full of all sorts of gifts from the pious villagers. Then, keeping their eyes devoutly downcast and their faces gravely virtuous, they bowed humble thanks as they made their way slowly back to the edge of the town. There the men changed their clothes and discreetly bought several flasks of *sraa* from a farmwife. They returned to the forest in high spirits and shamelessly drank all night.

After a few days of gluttonous eating and drinking, they had nothing left. Once more they put on their stolen monastery robes and decided to try their luck in another village. They walked smartly along the road, laughing and joking as they confidently planned ways to trick another group of simple villagers. As they approached the outskirts of the town, they saw a beautiful purple-leafed mango tree branching splendidly over a large clearing.

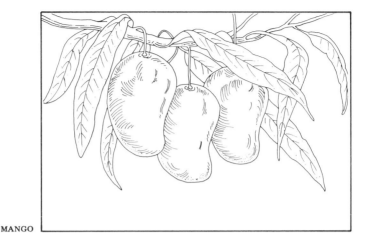

MANGO

"Ah! I have an excellent idea," Tah Tyen exclaimed. "Watch me closely."

He then carefully arranged his yellow robes around himself, sat down under the tree, and crossed his legs as if he were a meditation monk. "Now," he told the other three men, "go to the village and tell the people that a very holy monk has just stopped to rest near their village. And tell them all the other fine things we talked about."

And so the three, dressed as novices, walked through the streets of the town calling loudly to passersby, "O dear brothers! A holy meditation monk is resting under that old mango tree near your village. He loves you all very much. That is why he is here. He can pray with magic and cure all your sickness. He can save you. He can bring you luck and success. You should pay respect to him with tea and sugar and rice. Hurry! Very soon he must be on his way again."

The people believed the impostors. They excitedly gathered all sorts of teas and fruit and, hoping for great miracles, eagerly rushed to the old mango tree. There they offered their gifts with much reverence to Tah Tyen and asked him to pray for their good luck and great riches.

"From where do you come, most Venerable Sir?" one of the villagers asked.

"I come from the capital, my dear man," Tah Tyen solemnly answered. "But for a long time I have been practicing my meditations in the forest. I never leave my forest now and I never speak to anyone. But just last night, I dreamed that a great evil will happen in this district. So I decided that I must come here to try to save you all."

The surprised villagers heard Tah Tyen's prophecy of tragedy and were quite shaken. "Reverend Sir," a young man asked, "are you sure that something terrible will happen to us? What you say makes us tremble. We have not heard about these dreadful things."

Tah Tyen lowered his eyes still more and answered gravely, "My very dear people, as I was sitting in meditation last night, I saw terrible things that will come to you in seven days. Seven days from now something very dangerous will happen. I see floods and waters and lightning and great thunder. And all of you and all of your district will be destroyed. I love you all so dearly that my heart is filled with sorrow for you. I have come here to try to save you and to destroy that evil thing that would harm you."

The villagers fell into a panic. Some started to run away. Some sank to the ground. A few found their voices and, trembling, asked Tah Tyen, "Venerable Sir, should we move our houses? We could run from here and then be out of danger. But where should we go? What people will take us in? Where will we find land to grow our food? What shall we do, most holy Reverend?"

Tah Tyen raised his hand, "Let me sit in silence here and meditate. My meditations will tell us what to do."

Then Tah Tyen burned incense and candles. He drooped his head and sat with his eyes closed for a few minutes. When he rose up, he clasped his hands and, gazing beyond the people, announced, "Now I understand how to destroy such evil. But I need many things to do this."

"Oh, do not worry," the relieved villagers said. "We will give you whatever you need. We don't care about the cost. We only care about our lives. Please tell us what to do. We will do anything you tell us."

"Ah, my dear friends," Tah Tyen replied. "I am a holy Buddhist monk. It is very hard for me to tell you how to destroy the evil ghosts that are going to bring such disaster upon you, because the ghosts like to drink *sraa* and they like to boil chickens and they like to eat at night. I am very holy and I am forbidden to touch *sraa* or kill animals or even touch food at night."

The villagers rushed to assure Tah Tyen. "O Venerable Sir, you must not worry about these things. You only tell us what to do and we will prepare everything exactly as you say. We must help you destroy the evil ghosts."

Tah Tyen praised the villagers for their good sense and understanding. Then he told them that it would be necessary to build a small shelter for the ghosts near the mango tree. The grateful villagers followed Tah Tyen's instructions, and within a few hours a small cottage was completed. Next, Tah Tyen ordered the people to bring their golden statues of Buddha and all the jeweled ornaments from the temple to make an altar for the magic ceremonies. Then Tah Tyen and his three followers took a piece of cotton string and, chanting mantras, made a circle seven times around the cottage.

"Do not touch this cotton string," Tah Tyen warned the villagers. "It is a magic circle. You must stay outside this circle. If anyone comes within this circle or comes into the cottage, he will become mad and die instantly. Now, all of you, go home! Hurry! Bring us a lot of *sraa* and boiled chickens for the evil ghosts. Leave everything outside the magic circle. Then you must go quickly away. If the ghosts see you, they will kill you."

The villagers gladly obeyed Tah Tyen. They hurried to prepare the *sraa* and chickens and warned their children, "Stay away from that cottage. Never go inside the magic circle. If you do not listen, a terrible beast will eat you!"

That night when everything was quiet, Tah Tyen and his three disciples carefully crept to the string circle and took the chickens and *sraa* inside the cottage. They gorged themselves on the juicy chickens and got drunk on the *sraa*. And, the more they drank, the more loudly they talked and joked.

A few evenings later, a buffalo boy called Chow Saun was taking his buffaloes home from the field. He happened to walk near the cottage and he heard the voices of the four scoundrels. He thought to himself, "That sounds like many people are drunk in the magic cottage. Who is in there? I must go see with my own eyes. My mother and father have told me that I will become mad or die if I go near the circle. But it does not matter. I must see what is happening in there."

Then Chow Saun walked slowly, slowly to the thatched wall of the cottage. He carefully picked up a palm leaf covering a window opening and he peeked inside. There he saw the four men sitting in filthy clothes, outrageously guzzling *sraa* and roaring with laughter.

"Oh!" he gasped. "These are not monks. These are bad men! To eat chicken at night and to drink *sraa* like that!

My parents must be mad. We must not trust people like this anymore. They just eat our food and get drunk. I must go and tell my mother about this!"

Chow Saun forgot about his buffaloes and ran home. "Mother, Mother!" he called. "Where did you get such meditation monks? I just saw them eating chickens and getting drunk."

Chow Saun's mother heard him but she did not believe him. She was sure that he had become mad because he walked into the magic circle. "Oh, my dearest son," she cried. "The holy teacher warned us not to walk in the magic circle. Now you are mad. Who can save my son?"

Chow Saun protested, "No, no, Mother. I am not mad. I have seen this with my own eyes. These four bad men came to cheat us and take our food and money from us."

Chow Saun's mother did not listen to him at all. She clasped her hands and despaired, "Oh, my son is mad. What shall I do?"

Their neighbors, hearing Chow Saun shouting and his mother wailing, came to see what the trouble was. The poor woman cried to them, "My son walked into the magic circle and he became mad. Please help me. What shall I do? My son is completely mad."

The neighbors were horrified. Then they told his mother that the only one who could possibly cure Chow Saun would be the holy teacher himself. Chow Saun became quite angry as he listened to them. He cried because he was so young that no one believed him. But his mother, fearing that he would die, ran quickly to the cottage near the old mango tree. She stood outside the magic circle and called to Tah Tyen, "O Reverend Sir! Please help me. Please come out. An accident has happened!"

When Tah Tyen heard the woman's calls, he quickly wiped his greasy mouth and put on his saffron-yellow robe. Taking his walking stick in his hand, he poked his head through the window. "What has happened, madam? You look so upset."

The distraught woman knelt down respectfully. "Sir, my son Chow Saun came close to your cottage and now he is mad and he says that all our people are mad."

"Mother," Tah Tyen slowly replied, "I have forbidden your children to come to this cottage. If any child comes to this cottage, evil things will happen. Do you believe me? Tell me, dear woman, where is your son?"

"He is at home, Reverend Sir." the woman sobbed.

"Bring him here at once," Tah Tyen ordered. "I will try to cure his madness for you. The evil spirits in him came from this holy ceremony cottage. So now you must bring him back to the cottage to save him."

The woman returned home and begged all her relatives to look for Chow Saun and bring him to the holy men. They found the boy hiding under the floor of one of the bamboo houses. They pulled him out and held him tightly. He cried and struggled against their grip. He pleaded with them and told them that they had been tricked. But no one believed him because he was only a small buffalo boy. And so they carried him, still struggling and crying, to the edge of the cotton circle around the ceremony cottage.

Tah Tyen and his three disciples were waiting. As they took the crying boy into the cottage, Tah Tyen told the village men, "This poor boy is mad because a ghost is in possession of his body. I will mix holy water with magic herbs for the evil spirits. Then I will chant holy mantras and remove the ghosts from his body. Do not worry, he will be better tomorrow. Leave him now. Everyone must go home."

When the village men left, Tah Tyen and the other three men tied Chow Saun to the post in the center of the cottage. Then they beat him with large palm-leaf sticks and shouted, "Hey, you miserable sneaky monkey! What did you tell your mother?"

Chow Saun stolidly answered them, "I saw you! I saw you all drinking *sraa* and eating chicken at night."

The imposters were furious. They beat Chow Saun again. Even though he ached all over, he continued to cry out, "I did see you! I did see you!"

And they beat him again. Chow Saun began to feel that it was useless to fight these four strong men anymore. He thought to himself, "They are all mad in the village. I am all alone. These thieves have me tied up. I cannot do anything. It would be better if I stopped fighting."

Chow Saun lifted this face and whispered, "Reverend Sir, please forgive me. The ghosts made me mad. They made me see mad things. Now I am better. I know now it was the ghosts tricking me. I did not see you drinking *sraa*. I will not say this anymore."

The imposters dropped their sticks, and Tah Tyen told

the boy, "Of course, if you are no longer mad and if you understand that we holy men do not drink *sraa,* then we will untie you."

"Yes, sir," Chow Saun agreed. "Yes, sir. Please untie me. I promise not to say anything bad about you anymore."

When they untied Chow Saun, they told him he could not go home right away. For causing so much trouble, he would have to work as a servant for seven days. The poor boy was so exhausted that he curled up in a corner of the cottage and fell soundly asleep.

As he slept, the scoundrels made their plans. "We cannot stay here any longer," Tah Tyen told the other three. "More people will begin to suspect us. Let us take everything—the *sraa,* the chickens, and the gold and jewels from the altar—and run quickly back to the forest."

The next morning when Chow Saun awoke, he found everything gone. The cottage was empty. He looked to the altar. The golden Buddha and the jewels were all gone. He got up and sadly went home. Some old villagers saw him and called out, "Saun, you are better now. How do you feel?"

Chow Saun shook his head and quietly replied, "I do not feel good, my grandparents. And all of you will feel bad, too. You believed those rascal monks and you gave everything to them. Now they are gone and they took everything with them. If you do not believe me now, just come back with me to the ceremony cottage."

The old people called to the other villagers, and together

they all walked to the ceremony cottage near the mango tree. Everything was gone, and the villagers could do nothing.

When Cambodians address each other, they often put before the other person's name a title such as "Grandfather," even if the other person is not a member of the family. "Tah" means "grandfather" or "old man," but it can be used as well before the name of a lazy person who is not so old, as in the case of Tah Tyen in this story. "Chow" means "grandson," but it is used by older people to address any young boy.

The Polecat and
the Rooster

Once there was a hungry polecat who decided to leave the forest to find food in a nearby village. He soundlessly padded his slender body through the fields, carefully sniffing the air for the smell of food. Through the evening darkness, he soon caught a delicious whiff of some tasty bird. The polecat looked up and there, perched upon a limb of a tree, sat a rooster sleeping with his head tucked into his ruffled feathers.

Now, the polecat wanted to eat the rooster, but he could not climb the tree. So he decided to try to trick the rooster into coming down. The polecat crouched his body close to the tree trunk and gently called up to the rooster, "Hey, dear friend, wake up! I bring you a special message from our Supreme Lord. Our Lord says that from now on, all animals who have hated each other must become friends and never fight again. We must all live happily together in peace and harmony. So let us both begin our friendship now. Come down from your perch so that you and I can embrace each other just like peaceful, loving brothers."

When the rooster heard the polecat's voice, he woke up quickly. He looked sharply down upon his cunning old enemy whose slinky body crouched against the tree trunk. Now, the rooster had always been a sensible bird, and he just did not trust that old polecat. He thought awhile and then he slowly replied, "My dear brother Polecat, your message from our Lord is very beautiful. Yes, we should love each other and live in peace and friendship. I want to come down and make peace with you. But could you wait a few minutes, please? My friend, the dog, lives together with me here. He went out to the forest to find some food. Let us wait for him to return. Then I will come down from the tree and the three of us can celebrate our new friendship together."

Then the rooster stretched his body and opened his wings. He turned to the north and called loudly into the forest, "Hello-o, dear Dog, hello-o! Come home now! Our friend the polecat is waiting for you here!"

When there was no answer from the forest, the rooster called still more loudly, "Hello, hello-o, Dog! Can you hear me? Please come right now. Our friend the polecat is waiting."

The wary polecat thought he heard the dog coming. He was fearful because the dog was his old enemy. So he began to slip his soft body away from the tree.

The rooster pouted. "Oh, dear Polecat, don't go," he said. "Please wait. Our friend the dog will be here soon."

But the polecat fidgeted and cringed. "No, I cannot wait any longer. I must bring the message of the Supreme Lord to all the other animals."

And with that, the polecat scurried back into the forest. The rooster watched him go and then, settling his feathers, went back to sleep again.

In Buddhist traditions, people were often reborn as animals. Therefore, animals often talked and behaved just like ordinary people. Cambodian Buddhist monks used this story as an example of how clever reasoning can outwit scoundrels.

The Chief Monk of
the Monastery of Sohtan Koh

Where the Mekong River turns to the north in Kompong Cham Province sits the lovely island of Sohtan Koh. On this island long ago, Buddhist monks built their monastery. The Monastery of Sohtan Koh became famous as a great center of learning and as a place where all people could go for consolation and hope.

The good monks at the monastery followed the Ten Precepts of Buddhism. They lived a life of prayer, learning, and teaching. They wanted nothing for themselves and owned only their robes, alms bowl, needle, and water strainer. Grateful lay devotees supported the monks with gifts of food and money. According to Buddhist traditions, these gifts were "good deeds" that helped prepare the giver for a better life when he was reborn.

Many years ago, there was a chief monk of the Monastery of Sohtan Koh who was not quite content with his simple life. Each day as he sat in meditation, he would look at his hands folded upon his coarse yellow robe and sigh, "Ah, this life is so difficult. I have nothing here but my old alms bowl, a broken needle, and a rusty water strainer. If only I had a fine silk robe—a beautiful *cheyporh* made of soft shimmering brocade from Shanghai. Ah, then I could touch it and my fingers would smooth the silken folds as I pray. Oh, then I would feel so much better."

Now, at this time, across the river in the Chihe District there lived a lazy rascal called Sao. One day when Sao was sitting in a Chinese restaurant, he overheard a rich merchant boasting that he had just given a present of fifty *riel* to the Monastery of Sohtan Koh. "Hmm," thought Sao to himself. "If only I could find a way to get those fifty *riel!* What a good time I would have!"

Sao mulled over all his old tricks for a while and decided upon a plan. First, he hurried to an alley behind a Chinese laundry and easily stole some fine clothes from the carts. Then he quickly hid in a doorway and slipped on the clothes, making himself look like a prosperous businessman. So dressed, he sauntered down to the docks and hired a boat to take him to the island monastery. There, he respectfully bowed to the Buddhist novices and asked to speak with the chief monk. The novices, thinking that he was a wealthy lay devotee, quickly took him to the chief monk. And the monk, always happy to see a rich merchant visit the island, greeted Sao warmly.

Bowing very low, Sao began, "Venerable Sir, my mother's birthday is in this dry season. Her humble wish is that you perform a religious ceremony for her with incense, flowers, and candles. And for this, I will present a gift to you of new robes to wear for her special birthday blessing. My brother and his sons and my wife all agree that we should give you a beautiful gift of a fine new *cheyporh, angsakh,* and *spong.* Please, Venerable Sir, would you come with me to the market to choose the silk?"

The chief monk listened to the wily rascal's words and was absolutely delighted. Although he kept his face and body still and calm, he was just bursting with excitement at the thought of the fine silk robes. "Well, my son," he answered smoothly, "we have some old silk robes which we do not much like. If your mother wishes us to have such a gift, we must help you. I know of a Chinese silk-merchant in the Rokar Kao marketplace."

With his head still bowed low, almost touching the ground, Sao replied agreeably, "Venerable Sir, please show me this market, and I will buy you whatever you like."

The chief monk called his disciples to prepare his boat, and they rowed straightaway to the other side of the river to the Rokar Kao marketplace. When they arrived at the silk shop, the Chinese merchant respectfully welcomed them. "What would you want of us?" he asked.

The chief monk answered, "This lay devotee wishes to buy some fine silk from Shanghai to make us a gift of a robe. Please show us what you have."

The merchant took several bolts of silk from his shelves, untied them, and spread the elegant fabrics before the monk. The chief monk carefully touched each delicate piece and then, turning to Sao, said, "These two kinds would be the best for a monk's robes."

"Thank you, Venerable Sir," bowed Sao. Then the rascal said to the merchant, "Please give me fifty *riel*'s worth of these handsome silks."

With that, Sao reached into his wallet and pulled out twenty *riel*. "Oh!" he exclaimed. "I have only twenty *riel* with me. This is very bad. But I have a brother in the upper district who will lend me more money. Forgive me, Venerable Sir. I will hurry to my brother and come back soon. Please wait for me here."

Bowing briefly, Sao left the chief monk and the Chinese merchant. He walked quickly to the docks, where he found the disciples waiting in the rowboat. "Hey there!" he called to them. "The Venerable One orders you to take me back to the monastery. He needs fifty *riel* to pay for his purchases."

The disciples obediently rowed Sao back to the island. Once there, Sao shouted roughly to the novices, "Quickly, quickly now! Your chief monk orders you to give me fifty *riel* to pay the Chinese merchant for his goods."

The novices believed everything that Sao said because he looked like a wealthy businessman and because the chief monk had befriended him. They gave him the money, and then Sao and the disciples rowed back across the river. When they arrived at the docks, Sao told the disciples, "You wait here now. I will take the money to the Venerable One."

Sao walked easily away from the docks with the money in his pockets. He bought a few things that he wanted in the market. Then he headed for a village at the edge of the forest where he knew he could safely hide for a few weeks.

Meanwhile, the chief monk sat in the silk store and waited for Sao to return. Hours went by. The Chinese merchant kindly prepared many pots of tea with sugar for his respected visitor. Evening came and still Sao did not return. The chief monk was very annoyed. Finally, after telling the merchant to return the bolts of silk to the shelves, he left the store. He took himself back to the docks and snapped at his disciples, "Row back now. That evil devotee left me in the store and never returned! He went to borrow money from his brother for my silk robes. We have wasted a whole day waiting for him!"

Upon hearing their teacher, the disciples were puzzled. "O Venerable Sir," one of them said, "that devotee came right back here and told us that you ordered him to return to our monastery to get fifty *riel* to pay the Chinese for your silk. Then he told us to wait here, and he left to give you the money."

The chief monk groaned. "Stupid boys!" he shouted at them. "I did not order him to take the monastery money. He said that he was going to borrow money from his brother. You fools! Why do you believe such a liar? Oh, all of my money is gone and my pocket is broken!"

The disciples replied, "Respected Sir, we believed him because we saw that you were happy with him."

The chief monk angrily told his disciples to row quickly because the night was coming soon and it was the time of the typhoons.

The Buddha taught that people should not be greedy. Monks especially must follow the Ten Precepts of Buddhism, one of which forbids monks to take money or to adorn themselves with expensive clothing or ornaments.

A monk's clothes consist of three items: a *cheyporh,* or outer robe; an *angsakh,* an apron with pockets for carrying things; and a *spong,* or loincloth. His three possessions are an alms bowl for collecting money, a needle for sewing tears in his robes, and a strainer to strain dirty water for drinking.

In order for monks to live their lives and to see to the upkeep of their monasteries, they need the support of the people. Believers in Buddhism who support the monks are called "lay devotees."

The Story of
Chow Prak and Chow Lok

A few years ago, in Battambang Province near the Thai border, there were two buffalo boys who worked for the mayor. One of them, who was called Chow Prak, hated to work and was very unhappy that he had earned only two hundred *baht* in his entire lifetime. Each night as he fell asleep, he tried to think of ways to steal money and become rich.

One day when Chow Prak really did not feel like working at all, he said to the other buffalo boy, "We work hard taking care of these buffaloes from early morning till late at night, but the mayor does not send us enough food. If you take care of the buffaloes by yourself for a few days, I will go to the city and try to find a job. Then I will come back with a lot of good food for both of us."

The other buffalo boy agreed. So Chow Prak gathered

his pack and started on his way to the Sting District. After a few hours, he met a rascal, Nay Cha, who happened to be a Moslem. Nay Cha was also on his way to the Sting District. He thought that he would stay with his brother-in-law Nay Ou for a few weeks. So the two, Chow Prak and Nay Cha, walked the road together and soon arrived in the Sting District. Brother-in-law Nay Ou welcomed them and generously treated them both as honored guests in his home.

After a few days of lazy living, Nay Cha said to Chow Prak, "This is boring! We have no money to do anything! But I have an idea. If we sell ourselves to someone as servants, we can run away the next day and share the money."

Chow Prak thought that was a splendid idea. "Nay Cha," he said excitedly, "you are clever! Let's go! I'll walk behind you and act like your servant. We will walk to the marketplace and try to find someone who will buy me from you."

So the two rascals set off for the marketplace. There they heard that a farmer called Chow Lok needed another servant to help harvest the rice. "Ah, what luck!" said Chow Prak. "This farmer knew me as a good buffalo boy. I will make up some sort of sad story and beg him to buy me from you. Let's go talk to him."

The rascals found Chow Lok at home. He immediately recognized Chow Prak the buffalo boy. "Well, my boy Prak," the good farmer asked, "where are you living nowadays?"

Chow Prak made a sad face and answered, "Sir, nowadays I am Nay Cha's servant. But he is returning to his home in Phnom Penh and he says that I must go with him. Phnom Penh is so far from here, where I have always lived. I do not want to go. Please buy me from him so that I may stay here where my home has always been. If you pity me, please give Nay Cha one hundred *baht*. Then he can buy himself another servant in Phnom Penh."

Chow Lok took pity on the buffalo boy and gave one hundred *baht* to Nay Cha, who stuffed the money into his pack. Now, Chow Lok was a good businessman, so he asked Nay Cha for Chow Prak's servant papers. "Do not worry, Chow Lok," Nay Cha reassured him. "I will go to the city offices and bring you the official papers tomorrow."

Then Nay Cha put his arm around Prak's shoulder as if to say good-bye and whispered in his ear, "Meet me tomorrow morning at my brother-in-law's house and then we will divide this money."

And with that, Nay Cha quickly left the farmer's house thinking to himself, "Ah, good! Now I have all the money. Let Prak take care of himself. I must get away from the Thai border and get out of this district quickly."

Nay Cha hitched a ride on an oxcart with a merchant who was taking his goods to the Svay Por market. At the market, Nay Cha changed his Thai *baht* into Cambodian *riel*. He bought himself some new clothes, some good food, and some areca leaves to chew with his betal leaves. That night, Nay Cha took a riverboat across the Bakprea River to the Khleng District.

The next morning, Chow Prak prepared Chow Lok's breakfast and said to him, "Kind sir, I really do not wish to be anybody's servant anymore. Please understand. I have a brother in this Sting District who will lend me money to buy myself out of slavery. Please let me go to him and I will return to you before lunch time."

The kindly farmer agreed. Chow Prak hurried away to Brother-in-law Nay Ou's house. But Nay Ou had not seen Nay Cha for almost two days. Chow Prak was furious. "Stupid me!" he thought to himself. "Nay Cha took all the money and disappeared. I'll find him if it's the last thing I do!"

So Chow Prak began asking everyone in the district about Nay Cha. One villager, who had just returned from the Svay Por market, told Prak that he had seen Nay Cha taking a riverboat to the Khleng District. Chow Prak

gritted his teeth in anger and quickly headed for the road to the Bakprea River port.

Meanwhile, Chow Lok waited and waited for Chow Prak's return. When the former buffalo boy did not come back, Chow Lok became very angry. He knew that the buffalo boy had worked for the mayor. So he decided to walk to the Thai border to the mayor's office to ask about Chow Prak. There he learned that the second buffalo boy had also been waiting many days for Chow Prak to return. When the mayor heard that Chow Prak had left his buffalo work to lie and cheat and steal in the Sting District, he became furious. "Oh, that rascal!" he exclaimed. "I will catch him and punish him so! He will never lie and cheat and steal again!"

The mayor sent all of his servants to find Chow Prak. And in a short time they did find him—sitting in a Chinese restaurant waiting for the next riverboat to the Khleng District. They arrested him, put him in handcuffs, and brought him back to the mayor. As punishment, the mayor ordered Chow Prak to dig the weeds around the house every day for five years with his feet cuffed together to make sure that he could not run away. And each day as Chow Prak worked, he bitterly wailed that he did not steal any money. Nay Cha had all the money and Nay Cha was probably spending it somewhere in the Khleng District and having a good time.

Chow Lok, the good farmer, really was convinced that his money was hidden in Brother-in-law Nay Ou's house. So Chow Lok hired a lawyer, brought Nay Ou to court, and pleaded with the judge to make Nay Ou return the one hundred *baht* that he was hiding for Nay Cha and Chow Prak. Nay Ou told the judge that even though the two rascals had stayed in his house, he never saw the money. The judge really did not believe Nay Ou, since Nay Ou was a Moslem. However, the judge said he would think about it. And while he was thinking about the case, Nay Ou had to give one hundred *baht* to the mayor as security until the case was finally decided.

Nay Ou protested loudly about the injustice of it all. But if he did not follow the court's orders, he would be put in jail. So Nay Ou reluctantly gave the mayor the one hundred *baht*.

Now, the mayor had a girlfriend who was always asking him for money to buy expensive clothes, perfumes, and hashish. A few days after the mayor received the one hundred *baht*, he lent it to this girlfriend, who promptly spent it all buying more clothes, perfumes, and hashish.

At the end of a week, the judge finally made his decision. He called Nay Ou and Chow Lok into the court. "I have thought this matter over carefully," he solemnly stated, "and I have decided that the money was definitely hidden in the Moslem Nay Ou's house. And you, dear Chow Lok, since you are a good Buddhist, you should not be cheated. Go to our good mayor's office and collect your one hundred *baht*."

Chow Lok was overjoyed. He ran quickly to the mayor's office to collect his money. "Ah, my dear Chow Lok," the mayor greeted him. "Unfortunately, I had a little accident and the money is not here right now. Come back in a few days and I will have it then."

Every few days, Chow Lok went to the mayor's office and asked for his money. And every time the mayor had another excuse. Months went by like this. Chow Lok could not take the mayor to court, because the mayor was a high official. So the good farmer never did get his money back. And Chow Prak the buffalo boy continued to weed the mayor's gardens with his feet cuffed, and Nay Cha never did get caught.

Cambodian monks constantly preached against foolish, greedy people. In this slapstick comedy, no one wins because no one really deserves to win. The one rascal who escapes will certainly get his just deserts in his next life when he is reborn.

The setting of this story, Battambang Province, is now a part of Cambodia, but at the time of the story (about one hundred years ago), it belonged to Thailand.

More than ninety percent of the Cambodian people are Buddhists. As we can see in this story, there was often prejudice against Moslems, a religious minority in Cambodia.

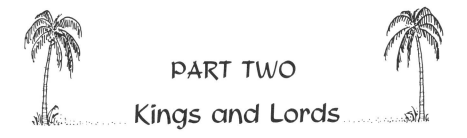

PART TWO
Kings and Lords

The Story
of the Eagle of Iso

Iso Ishvara, the High Sovereign Lord, had a beautiful eagle whom he truly adored. He lavishly indulged the eagle's every whim and utterly believed anything this bird told him. Now, this pampered pet had an outrageous appetite and was quite shameless in taking advantage of Lord Iso's generous love. Whenever the eagle hungered for a particular animal, he would come before Iso, bow down gravely, and murmur, "I dreamed that I must eat a lovely buffalo for dinner," or, "I dreamed that I must eat a delicious mongoose for lunch." Lord Iso would always believe his beloved eagle's dreams and would promptly summon each of the animals in turn to come at once to the mountain so that the eagle could eat them. All of the animals in the forest lived in terror of the gluttonous eagle, but they dared not protest, because they feared the anger of the powerful Iso, who controlled all the world.

One day, the eagle thought that he would like to eat a white elephant, so he once again slyly announced to Iso, "I dreamed that I must eat a white elephant." Upon hearing this, Lord Iso immediately sent his servant to command the white elephant mother and her son to cleanse themselves and to come straightaway to the mountain, because the beautiful eagle dreamed that he must eat them.

When the white elephant mother and son heard that the eagle wished to eat them, they cried with grief and great despair. They were terrified of dying and they knew no one could help them. Distraught, they went down to the lake to wash themselves. An owl, sitting on the branch of an areca tree, saw the white elephant mother and son stumbling along and crying pitifully. He called to them, "Hey! White Elephant, why are you sobbing like that?"

The white elephant mother sorrowfully told the owl her sad story from the beginning to the end. The owl listened and then muttered, "Oh, that Lord Iso! Why is he so unjust! Why does he believe that rascal eagle and let him torment all the animals like that?"

The white elephant mother tearfully pleaded, "Owl, I cannot find anyone to help us. Please save our lives. If you save us, we will stay with you always and serve you faithfully forever."

The owl had a great compassion for the white elephant mother and son. "All right," he agreed. "Now you are my servants. I will go to bargain with Iso Ishvara and try to save your lives."

The great white elephant mother told the owl to sit upon her head, and together the three proceeded to the mountain of the Sovereign Lord Iso. When they reached that place, the owl flew down from his perch on the elephant's head and settled himself close to the throne of Iso. "O Lord of All This World," the owl began plaintively, "this white elephant mother and son are my servants. Why did you summon them here to die? What is the matter with you, Lord?"

"Owl," Iso impatiently replied, "your servants will die today because my eagle dreamed that he must eat your white elephants. That is the reason I summoned them to the mountain."

Then the owl sadly folded his feathers and asked, "Lord! Do you believe the eagle's dreams? Are you sure that the eagle's dreams must come true?"

"Owl," Iso indignantly replied, "whatever this eagle dreams, I believe. His dreams always must come true. Of this I am certain."

"Oh, of course, Lord," said the owl quickly. "I respect you absolutely. If you believe your eagle's dreams, then I believe your eagle's dreams. Now I know why my elephants must die today. I agree with you—your eagle must eat my elephants." The owl stopped for a moment and yawned sleepily. Then he apologized, "Please forgive me, Supreme Lord. But last night I was so busy catching crabs to eat that I did not sleep very much. Please let me sleep for a few minutes, and then I will take my white elephant mother and her son to your eagle."

So speaking, the owl nodded, closed his eyes, and fell sound asleep. After a few minutes, he awakened, slowly stretched his body, and preened his feathers. A soft smile spread contentedly across his face.

Iso saw the owl's dreamy happiness and asked, "What is the matter with you, Owl? What makes you look so happy now?"

"Lord," the owl replied, "just now while I was sleeping, I had a very pleasant dream. I think that this dream will bring me good fortune, Lord."

Upon hearing this, Lord Iso became very curious. "What on earth did you dream about, Owl? Tell me," he urged.

"Oh, no!" the owl fretted. "My dream was so strange—so very strange. I dare not tell you, Lord."

"Oh, come now," Iso coaxed. "Please tell me your dream."

The owl hesitated for a moment and then began to speak again. "I dreamed that your wife, Oma Phogavatt, loved me so much that you, Lord Iso, agreed that we should be married. Supreme Lord, I believe my dreams. And, my dreams always must come true. Of this I am certain. So now, Lord, please call Oma Phogavatt to come to me here so that we may be married."

Upon hearing the owl's dream, the Supreme Lord Iso became quite irritated. "Your dream is nonsense!" he angrily exclaimed. "We could never believe that your dreams must come true, you foolish fellow!"

The owl gazed patiently at the Supreme Lord and wearily murmured, "Lord, you say that you cannot believe my dream and that my dreams cannot come true. What about your eagle's dream? Why do you believe his dream and say that his dreams must come true? Please act with the same justice for both of us, because both of us are animals."

Iso Ishvara listened thoughtfully to the owl's logical reasoning and could not think of any argument to defend himself. Reluctantly he grumbled, "All right. You may take your white elephant mother and son away from here. We forgive them for your sake."

The owl bowed and said, "Good-bye, Lord." Then the owl peacefully led the white elephant mother and son home.

Iso Ishvara was the highest god who ruled over other gods. He was worshiped by the Indian Hindus (who called him Siva) and by Buddhists of some sects. However, he was often considered vain, unjust, and unreasonable (as he is in this story). The Cambodian monks told this story to josh him gently.

The Three Servants
of King Bimbisara

Long ago in the land of India, there lived the noble King Bimbisara, who ruled with compassion and justice. Now, this good king's only son, Prince Ajatasatru, was a brash and irresponsible young man. He resented his father's power and often wished that he himself were king.

One day, Devadatta, the evil cousin of Lord Buddha, came to live at the palace. Devadatta was also jealous of the great wealth and power of King Bimbisara. He was determined to find a way to grasp some of that wealth and power for himself. As Devadatta watched the behavior of the unhappy young prince, he decided to take advantage of the boy's reckless greed and impetuous anger.

Devadatta befriended the Royal Child. Each day, he accompanied the prince and his rowdy companions wherever they went. He flattered Prince Ajatasatru at every opportunity, praising his cleverness and fearlessness. He ruthlessly encouraged the boy's jealousy of his father by telling him vicious lies. He even told Ajatasatru that the king was planning to disinherit him and give the throne to a younger sister. Finally, Devadatta convinced the prince that he could easily kill his father and take over the kingdom.

So one morning, when the king's palace was closed to visitors, Ajatasatru secretly strapped a sharp dagger into his belt and strode to the courtyard gates. The chief of the Royal Guard saw the prince approaching and called out to him that the king forbade anyone to enter the palace grounds before noon. Arrogantly ignoring the guard, Ajatasatru grabbed the gate and threw it open. "You fool! I am the Royal Child!" he snapped at the guard.

The chief of the Royal Guard acted swiftly. He ordered his two officers to arrest Ajatasatru. The two guards bound his hands and feet. They searched him and found the hidden dagger used only for killing enemies.

The three guards now found themselves in a difficult situation. "Hmm. What should we do now?" the chief of the Royal Guard muttered. "King Bimbisara forbids anyone to enter his palace at this time. He forbids anyone to carry any weapon on the palace grounds. He ordered us to kill any criminal who does not obey these laws. So now we have arrested the Royal Child, who was carrying a dagger. The Royal Child is now a criminal. We must obey the king's orders. We have no choice. I say that we must find that slimy Devadatta and all of the prince's other traitorous friends. We must kill them and their families and anyone else who is plotting to kill the king."

The two officers of the Royal Guard listened to their chief, agreeing that this was a most delicate situation. But they were disturbed and confused. They were afraid to act rashly. The first officer said, "Yes, I agree that this is a criminal act. But we should kill only the Royal Child and perhaps Devadatta. We are not so sure that the prince's friends and their families knew about this plot. Perhaps we should wait and find out more before we kill them also."

Now, the second officer of the Royal Guard was a wise and deliberate man. He carefully considered the words of his friends and then he spoke. "The law of the land gives us the power to arrest and punish criminal acts of ordinary people. But this is the Royal Child. He is not an ordinary person. Ajatasatru is the beloved son of our king. We palace guards are only servants. We do not have the right to decide punishment for the Royal Child. Come, let us take this pitiful prince and his dagger to the king. King Bimbisara will act with wisdom and justice."

So they untied Ajatasatru's hands and feet and brought him before the king. The three guards told the king their story.

The great king sat with his face resting upon his hand and listened sadly to the tragedy of his son's treachery and to the proposals for judgment made by each of the guards. Then he wearily stood up and, straightening his robes, spoke to his three servants. "Chief of the Royal Guard, you wished to kill Devadatta, the Royal Child, and all his friends and their families. That is unreasonable. You are now immediately dismissed from the Royal Guard. Return to your village.

"First Officer of the Royal Guard, you wished to kill the Royal Child and Devadatta. It is not fitting for you to judge and condemn the royal family. You also are dismissed from the Royal Guard. Return to your former work of tending our water buffaloes.

"Second Officer of the Royal Guard, you wisely reasoned that each case must be judged according to the circumstances. Thank you for bringing my son back to me. You will now be chief of the Royal Guard. Together we will teach my son how to be a wise and noble king."

King Bimbisara ruled the Magadha kingdom near the Ganges River of India from 543 to 491 B.C. He was king at the time of the birth of Gautama, the Buddha. Bimbisara was the earliest Indian king who developed an efficient political administration and system of justice. His son, Ajatasatru, continued his father's system of government, ruling from 491 to 459 B.C.

The King
and the Poor Boy

In a small village near the edge of the forest, there once lived a buffalo boy who had no mother or father. His uncle, who was the chief cook for the king, pitied the poor boy. So he invited the boy to stay with him in the palace. The grateful boy worked hard to help his uncle. He washed the plates, polished the cups, cleaned the dining room tables, and mopped the floors. At the end of each month, his uncle gave him six *sen* as his wages.

Now the king frequently inspected the palace quarters. He often noticed the hardworking boy mopping the floors or polishing the cups, cheerfully and in good humor. One day the king asked the boy, "Do you receive wages for your hard work?"

The boy bowed and said, "Yes, I do, Your Majesty. I earn six *sen* every month."

Then the king asked, "Do you think you are rich or do you think you are poor?"

"Your Majesty," the boy replied, "I think that I am as rich as a king."

The king was taken by surprise. "Why is this poor boy talking such nonsense?" he mused to himself.

Once more, the king spoke to the boy, "I am a king and I have all the power and riches of this country. You earn only six *sen* a month. Why do you say you are as rich as I am?"

The boy laid down his broom and slowly replied to the king, "Your Majesty, I may receive only six *sen* each month, but I eat from one plate and you also eat from one plate. I sleep for one night and you also sleep for one night. We eat and sleep the same. There is no difference. Now, Your Majesty, do you understand why I say that I am as rich as a king?"

The king understood and was satisfied.

The Buddha preached about the equality of all human beings. In this story, a vain king, too proud of his wealth, is taught by his lowly servant that in the most important things of life, all men are equal brothers.

The Story
of Bhikkhu Sok

Many years ago, there was a great famine in Kampuchea. A Phnong man called Chow Phnong Kruu came down from his mountain village to the town to Senmonorom to try to find food for his family. When he returned home some time later, the superstitious villagers were afraid of him because he had dared to leave their secluded village and live boldly among the lowland strangers.

During the next few weeks, Chow Phnong Kruu began to show his family some of the new things that he had learned about cooking and preserving food. These new ways greatly disturbed the simple-living Phnongs. They began to whisper to each other that Chow was practicing evil magic.

Then one day, a neighbor's small child became ill and died. The villagers blamed Chow Phnong Kruu's magic for the child's death and demanded that the chief of the Phnongs punish him. Now, the chief of the Phnongs had forbidden his people to practice black magic. He was furious when he heard that Chow had disobeyed his orders. So the Phnong chief immediately sent for a group of hunters from the village and ordered them to kill Chow Phnong Kruu and all of his family with seven sharp razors.

The hunters did their job well. Within a few hours, Chow Phnong Kruu and all of his family were dead. All, that is, except for one small boy named Chow Sok. That morning, Chow Sok had been sent to the rice field at the edge of the forest to wait for the rice buds to ripen for harvesting. Late that afternoon, while he was camped there, he heard an angry group of hunters pass through behind the trees. He listened in horror as they spoke about the killings of his mother, his father, his grandparents, his sisters and brothers, his aunts and uncles—his entire family. He trembled with terror when the hunters grumbled impatiently that one small boy was still alive and no one could find him.

When the hunters had passed, Chow Sok quickly climbed to the top of a tall tree and hid himself in a thick tangle of liana vines. From the treetop, he watched as the hunters stomped through the rice field, searching along every crevice of the valley and in every pile of brushwood for the missing boy. When the sun set, the discouraged hunters turned back and headed for their village in the upper hills.

Sick with grief and fear, Chow Sok sat in the safe tangle of liana vines until the middle of the night. Then he slowly crept down from the tree and carefully made his way across the rice field, into the forest, and down to another Phnong village nestled in the lower hills.

At the edge of the village was a small hut with fruit in thickly woven baskets leaning against the doorway. Chow Sok was cold and tired and hungry. He ate some fruit and then, curling up between the baskets, fell asleep.

In the morning, the old man who lived alone in the hut saw the sleeping boy. He knew immediately that this must be the child that the hunters from the upper village had been looking for. The old man pitied the child. Waking the boy and warning him to be very quiet, the old man took him into the hut and hid him under some old straw mats.

Later that morning the hunters went down to the lower Phnong village to search again for the boy. When they saw the old man sitting in the doorway of his small hut,

they asked if he had seen any strangers in the village. He gazed at them with empty eyes and shook his head. The hunters supposed that the old man was too simple even to think of deceiving them. They looked at his musty palm-leaf hut and decided that it was too small for even one person. No one could possibly be hidden under its cracking, ramshackle roof. Besides, the boy had cleverly escaped them for almost two days. He certainly would not be foolish enough to try to hide in the first broken-down hut that was closest to the edge of the forest.

Deciding that it would be a waste of time to search the old man's hut, the hunters moved on to the larger huts in the center of the village. They searched all of the houses thoroughly and questioned all of the villagers sharply. No one had seen the missing boy.

When the hunters had gone, the old man spoke to the boy. "My little one," he said, "you must not stay here. The hunters will come back again. This house is too close to the upper village, where the chief of the Phnongs lives. It will not be peaceful here. Soon the villagers will know about you. If you want to save your life, you must go and live with the Kampucheans in the lowlands. Only this morning I saw a merchant's cart returning to the lands below. You must run quickly to catch up with him. Beg him to take you down to Kratieh Province."

Chow Sok listened to the old man. Then he put the palms of his hands together and, lifting them close to his forehead, bowed low to show the old man his great respect and gratitude. The old man gave him a small bundle of fruit, and Chow Sok quickly ran down the road to find the merchant from Kratieh.

Soon he saw the merchant with his oxcart piled high with brushwood and dried fish. Feeling too shy to speak to the merchant who came from a strange land, Chow Sok walked far behind the cart for a long time. Then, feeling very tired, he edged closer and jumped up to lie down on the *praek* of the cart. The oxcart swayed, and the merchant turned quickly to see the small Phnong boy hanging on behind the wheel.

"Hey there! Who are you, boy? Where are your parents? Why are you hanging on behind my oxcart?" he called out to the boy in the Phnong language.

The embarrassed child quickly scrambled down from the wooden *praek*. He timidly told the merchant the sad

ROOFED CART

story about his family, the chief's hunters, and the kindly old man.

The merchant understood everything and pitied the frightened boy. "Ah, my poor child," he said. "You must come with me away from the Phnong villages. You may live with me in Kratieh. I have always wanted a son. Come, come now. Jump up here with me on this wood pile and let us leave this place quickly."

They journeyed together safely and reached Kratieh in good time.

The merchant grew to love Chow Sok as dearly as if he were really his own son. He taught Chow Sok the Khmer language and the customs of the country. In turn, Chow Sok was completely devoted to his new-found father. He studied with great care and eagerly helped the merchant with all of his work.

After a few years, the merchant sent Chow Sok to study at the monastery school of Kratieh. The monks were impressed with the boy's keen mind and good character. When Chow Sok was fifteen years old, he was ordained as a novice. When he was twenty-one, the monks fully ordained him as a monk—a *bhikkhu*. He was now called Bhikkhu Sok.

Bhikkhu Sok became a noble and honored monk. His wisdom and justice were respected throughout the land.

High in the northeastern mountains of Cambodia live ancient tribes of people called Phnongs, who were perhaps the first inhabitants of the land many thousands of years ago. The Cambodians were prejudiced against these "different" people and usually treated them as dull-witted savages; in fact, the word *phnong* means "savage" in Cambodian.

Buddha, the Enlightened One, preached against the caste system of the Hindu Brahmans. People should not be prejudiced, he said. All men should treat each other with dignity. The monks used this story to attack people's prejudice against new ideas, to teach the Cambodians that the Phnongs were also human beings with common human emotions, and to prove that the Phnongs had the same abilities as anyone else to work hard and become successful.

The story mentions that Chow Sok was waiting for the rice buds to ripen. In the rice harvesting season, parents would send their young children to the fields to watch the grains of rice ripen from young green buds to golden seeds. The children were to tell their parents as soon as the buds turned golden—so that the rice could be harvested immediately, before birds could swoop down and eat the entire crop.

When Cambodians greet each other or wish to show gratitude to another person, as Chow Sok in the story does to the old man, they place the palms of their hands together. The higher the hands are raised, from the chest to the forehead, the greater is the respect shown to the other person.

The King and
the Buffalo Boy

Once long ago, a king and his ministers were hunting in the forest. They rode together for many hours, but they could not find any animals. Since they were tired and hungry, they all decided to stop and rest. The ministers ordered the servants to pitch the hunting tents and to prepare the special food for the king's lunch.

While the king was waiting for his lunch, he saw a small deer bound into the forest. He quickly spurred his horse on to chase the deer. The young horse galloped briskly after the deer, carrying the king up one path and down another. Soon they were deep in the forest, and the king knew he was lost. He quieted his sweating horse and tried to listen for the voices of his ministers and servants. The forest was very still. The king heard only the leaves of the trees moving slightly and a few birds calling to each other in the distance. He gently patted his horse and was guiding her slowly through the trees when he heard the voice of a young boy.

"Hello! Is anyone there?" the king called out.

"Yes!" came the answer. "It is me, the buffalo boy."

The king led his horse into the clearing, and the buffalo boy stepped out to greet him. "Hello, sir. Are you looking for me?"

The king thought it best to pretend that he was an ordinary man, so he spoke to the buffalo boy with simple words. "My dear boy, I am lost. My friends made their camp at the edge of this forest near two large pepper trees. I wandered into this forest with my horse and now I cannot find them."

"Sir," the buffalo boy said, "do not worry. I know that place very well. I will show you the way."

"Ah! That is good!" said the king. "Please come sit behind me on my horse and we will ride together."

The buffalo boy made sure his animals would be safe and then jumped up behind the king. He guided the king across the clearing and onto a hidden path under the spreading liana vines.

As they rode along, the king thought to himself, "This is a kind and hardworking boy. I like him. I wonder if he likes me, his king." Then the king asked, "My dear boy, do you know the king who rules this country?"

"I don't know what you mean," the puzzled boy answered. "My grandmother used to tell me stories about kings. But I really do not know what a king is. I've never seen a king. I don't even know where a king lives."

The king was a little taken aback. "Well, do you want to know what a king is? Would you like to meet a king?"

"Oh, that would be fun," replied the buffalo boy.

"All right!" the king said. "If you lead me out of the forest to meet my friends, I will give you money, and I will also show you a king. When we meet my friends, you watch everyone carefully. Any man who takes his hat off is not a king. Any man who keeps his hat on is a king. Remember now, if you watch carefully, you will know which man is a king."

The buffalo boy promised the king that he would watch everyone very carefully. Soon they arrived at the edge of the forest near the two large pepper trees. Now, all the ministers and servants had been terribly worried about the king. When they saw him riding safely out of the forest, they all jumped up and took off their hats.

The king turned around to the buffalo boy and proudly asked, "Now, my dear boy, do you know who is king?"

The overjoyed buffalo boy laughed. "Oh yes! There are two kings here. I am a king and you are a king!"

Some of the ministers who were standing nearby overheard the boy. "Hey, boy!" they scolded. "You are not the king. You must never dare say that again!"

"Oh," the buffalo boy protested. "This gentleman told me that anyone who does not take his hat off is king. I did not take my hat off, so I must be a king!"

The king was annoyed because his little game did not turn out as he had planned. He angrily ordered the boy to get down from the horse and to go back to his buffaloes. The poor boy, who really could not understand what had happened, looked up at the king and protested, "But sir, I did what you told me to. You promised to give me money if I helped you find your friends!"

Now the king was furious. "I have no money to give you!" he shouted. "You had better go home quickly or I will have you soundly beaten!"

So the buffalo boy turned away from the king and went back to his buffaloes.

Buddhists believed that a king, as a leader of his people, had an obligation to set a good example of morality for all his subjects to follow. But kings were human beings and, just like everyone else, imperfect. Monks told this story to teach the equality and imperfections of all people.

The Cambodian language had special words for the exclusive use of the king and his court. In this story, since the use of these words would identify the king as a royal person, he speaks to the buffalo boy with "simple words." The common people of Cambodia could use the special words only when addressing royalty.

The Story of
the Old Brahmani Lady

Once upon a time, a Bodhisattva was born as the son of a noble Brahman couple. Since his father died when this Bodhisattva was quite young, his mother sent him to the great teachers at the center of learning of Taxila to study the Vedas, the ancient scriptures.

After many years of diligent work, the Bodhisattva finished his studies and returned to the home of his mother, who was by now an old lady. The Bodhisattva cared for his aging mother and began to teach the knowledge found in the three Vedas to the good youths who lived in his district. The Bodhisattva was such a wise and compassionate teacher that he soon became famous. Scholars and students traveled from distant lands to listen to him and to learn from his great wisdom.

Among the Bodhisattva's many students was a young

man from a poor village who was so unusually handsome
that he dazzled the eyes of all who looked upon him. The
young man seemed unaware of his splendid beauty as
he studied the Vedas carefully and faithfully for three
years. At the end of this time, the youth had learned all
the knowledge of the Vedas. Bidding good-bye to his
kind teacher, the Bodhisattva, he returned to his village.

When he arrived home, the handsome youth told his
parents about the great wisdom he had learned. His
mother listened thoughtfully and then said, "I am proud
of your vast learning of the three Vedas—the Rig-Veda,
the Sama-Veda, and the Yajur-Veda. But tell me, have
you learned anything about the courting of women?"

The handsome boy shook his head. "No, Mother,"
he replied. "I have not yet learned anything about the
courting of women." So the youth returned to the Bodhisattva and asked to learn about women.

The Bodhisattva carefully considered the matter and
advised, "Of course, I do not know about this. But my
mother understands the courting of women very well.
You must study that knowledge with her. Go straight
to my house over there and ask her to teach you."

Thanking the Bodhisattva, the handsome boy went
to pay his respects to the Brahmani lady. This noble lady
was now more than eighty years old. Her skin was wrinkled
and her hands trembled with age. But when she saw the
handsome youth before her, she instantly fell in love with
him. Without even bothering to be mannerly, she declared,
"I love you very much and you must marry me."

"Oh!" the astonished youth faltered. "I cannot marry you, because you are the noble mother of my respected teacher. I honor him very much. And so I honor you very much. Since I am his student, I should not do anything discourteous that might distress him."

The old Brahmani lady lifted her trembling hand and wheedled, "Oh, my beautiful boy! Do not worry about my son. I will find a way to get rid of him. Perhaps I must even kill him."

The youth was very upset by the words of the old woman. He backed away slowly. His voice shaking, he said, "Yes, madam, if you dare to do such a thing to your own son, then I know that I must surely agree to marry you."

BODHISATTVA

Now, the youth loved his wise and compassionate teacher, and feared for his life. He quickly ran to the monastery and, with great embarrassment, told the Bodhisattva about the old Brahmani lady's irreverent proposals. The Bodhisattva pondered awhile and then gravely replied, "Of course, if my mother wishes to do away with me, you should ask her how she plans to do this. And, does she wish to do so at night or in the morning? Please, young man, go and ask her."

The young disciple went to see the old Brahmani lady again and asked her how she planned to get rid of the Bodhisattva. The aged woman eagerly explained her plans. "I will kill my son tonight. When he is sleeping, I will bring a sharp sword and cut off his head. But this must be a secret between us. You must never tell anyone, because after we are married, we must live peacefully together without any trouble."

Upon hearing this, the youth once more returned to the Bodhisattva and told him the details of the old lady's plans. The Bodhisattva listened thoughtfully and then carefully instructed the youth, "When night comes, I will bring a banana tree of about four arm-lengths and place it in my bed. Then I will place a blanket over this tree so that it will look like a man who is sleeping very soundly with his head covered. You will come with me tonight and see the nature of my mother's character."

Late that evening, the Bodhisattva and the young man prepared the bed with the covered banana tree. Then they stood quietly behind the curtain and waited. Soon everything grew still. In a little while, the old Brahmani lady entered the room dragging a large sword behind her. She walked slowly and softly to the Bodhisattva's bed. She touched the bed carefully to make sure that he slept soundly. Then she felt what she thought was his leg, and finally she placed her withered fingers lightly upon his head. When nothing moved, she was certain that her son was in a deep sleep. Since she knew that she was old, she summoned all her strength to lift the huge sword and brought it crashing down onto the covered banana tree. But the sword was so heavy that the great effort proved too much for her. As the sword fell onto the tree, the old Brahmani lady toppled over and died instantly.

The Bodhisattva and the handsome youth watched and understood. "Oh," they said. "Poor lady! She died because of love."

In the Hindu religion, the Brahmans were the highest noble caste, supposedly wiser and more privileged than anyone else. (Female members of this caste were called Brahmani.) Buddhist monks delighted in telling stories in which Brahmans were depicted as crude, selfish, and silly.

A Bodhisattva is a being who is able to enter nirvana (something like heaven) and experience the ultimate happiness, but who declines to do so in order to remain on earth and help others.

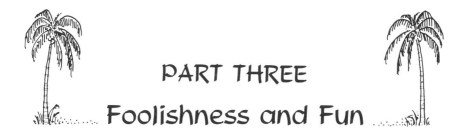

PART THREE
Foolishness and Fun

The Foolish Man
and the King's Minister

Once there was a foolish man who rode his buffalo to market with a basket of unhusked rice strapped upon the buffalo's back. The road was muddy and narrow, and the buffalo lumbered along with great difficulty. The foolish man gently prodded the beast onward and thought to himself, "Ah, my poor buffalo! I am so heavy and here I sit on his back. Then I pack this big basket of unhusked rice upon his back. What a great load! Ah, my poor buffalo. How he must be suffering!"

So they rode along, the buffalo swaying clumsily under his bulky load and the foolish man troubled by the suffering of the patient animal. After a while they came upon a small girl walking along between the paddies, balancing a basket of unhusked rice upon her head. "Aha! That's it!" exclaimed the foolish man. "If I put my basket of rice upon my head, then my poor buffalo will not have such a heavy load to carry!"

And with that, the foolish man placed the large basket upon his head, balancing it carefully with his hands as he sat upon his buffalo's back. From that day on, he always rode his buffalo from the fields to the market, carrying the basket of unhusked rice upon his head.

Now, at this time, the king of that country loved to be entertained by funny clowns and foolish jesters. One day when he became bored with their usual tricks, he called his supreme first minister to his side and said, "These dull buffoons make me tired with their same old tricks. Go out to the countryside and find some amusing fool who will make me laugh again. Bring him back to the palace and I will pay him well to entertain me."

So the supreme first minister saddled his horse and began to look for some silly man who would make the king

laugh again. Although he searched the countryside for many weeks, wandering from one place to another, he could not find any foolish man.

One day, the minister came to a rice field and saw a man riding upon his buffalo with a basket of unhusked rice balanced on his head. "Aha!" thought the minister to himself. "Now that man certainly looks foolish riding on a buffalo with a basket on his head. I never saw anything like that before. I bet that he could make the king really laugh."

So the minister prodded his horse to ride alongside the buffalo. "Hey!" he called to the man. "Why do you carry that heavy basket of rice on your head? Why don't you strap it on the buffalo's back? Are you a fool?"

"Sir, I am not a fool," the man replied. "I love my poor buffalo who works so hard for me. But I sit on his back and I am one heavy load. Now if I also set this heavy basket of rice on his back, my poor animal will have to carry two heavy loads. So that is why I carry the rice basket on my head. No sir, I am not a fool."

The minister listened thoughtfully to the man. Then he sympathetically replied, "Excuse me. Now I know that you are not a foolish man."

The supreme first minister rode back to the palace and went in to see the king. "Your Majesty," he reported, "I looked all over the kingdom but I could not find any foolish man to amuse you. I only found a kind man who sat on his buffalo and carried his heavy basket of rice upon his head to make the load easier for his poor animal."

The Bee and the Frog

Once there was a yellow bee who loved to slip from one flower to another sipping sweet nectar and gathering soft pollen. One day she met a fat frog sitting under a flower. "Hello, Frog," she buzzed. "Why are you just sitting there?"

"Oh," the frog boasted, "I am on my way to the Himalaya Mountains."

The yellow bee turned up her nose. "Fiddlesticks," she sneered. "How can you go to the Himalayas? Your legs are too short. I myself am on my way to the Himalayas. Can't you see how beautifully I fly?"

"Humph!" the frog retorted. "And I suppose you can fly there with your little wings?"

"My dear Frog," the yellow bee snapped back. "I can fly around the Himalayas seven times in one day!"

The frog puffed himself up. "That's nothing!" he

blustered. "I can go to the Himalayas in the morning and return home in the evening of the same day. Besides," he croaked, "what kind of useless animal would waste his time just flying around the Himalayas seven times in one day?"

"Well, indeed!" the bee bristled. "And I would like to know what kind of useless animal would waste his time just hopping to the Himalayas and back again in one day!"

Then the yellow bee stiffened her body and, leaning down close to the frog's ear, slowly hissed, "Anyway, my fine friend, when I was flying around the Himalayas all day yesterday, I did not see you there!"

The fat frog said nothing more, and the yellow bee flew away.

Modesty and humility are Buddhist virtues. Cambodian monks used this tale to teach the people that self-conceit should always be avoided.

A Father, a Son, and a Donkey

There was a man named Chow Khok who had a baby donkey. When the foal was fat, Chow Khok said to his son, "Our donkey is nice and fat now. He will bring us a good price at the market. But if we walk him all the way to the village on the far side of the river, he will grow thin and no one will want him. I think that we should tie him gently to a pole and carry him between our shoulders."

The son agreed. So they tied the donkey's four legs to the middle of a long bamboo pole. Then, placing the ends of the pole securely on their shoulders, they proceeded to march to the village with the donkey hanging upside down between them.

As they walked along the road, a group of people saw the threesome and began laughing. "Ho, ho, ho! What's this? Donkeys, horses, or pigs? Why are these stupid fellows carrying a donkey like a pig? Hey, both of you!

Are you crazy carrying a donkey on a pole on your shoulders? Why don't you get on his back and ride him?"

Chow Khok and his son heard the crowd's jeers and were greatly embarrassed. They discussed the matter together. "I suppose we must look rather strange to these people. Let's untie our donkey and get on him. But he is really too small for both of us to ride on his back. What shall we do?"

After thinking a bit, Chow Khok said to his son, "I know. You ride on the animal's back, since you are smaller, and I will walk behind and hold the packs and reins."

His son agreed. So they untied the donkey's legs and proceeded to the village, the son riding and the father walking behind holding the packs and the donkey's reins.

When they arrived at the edge of the village, some people called out to the son, "Hey, boy! Where are you going with your donkey?"

"We're riding to the market to sell him," the boy called back.

"Who is that old man with the reins walking behind you?" a villager asked.

"Oh," replied the son. "He is my father."

Then a villager scolded the boy. "You are an ungrateful son. You have no right to ride comfortably on that donkey and to drag your poor old father behind you like a servant. Get off and let your father ride."

The humiliated son turned to look at his father, who quickly whispered back, "Yes, yes. I will get on the donkey. You walk in front."

So the father mounted the donkey. Taking the reins
in his hand, the boy walked ahead. Soon they arrived
at the village well, where many girls were dipping water
for their families. Seeing the young boy walking tall in
front of the donkey, all the girls thought him quite handsome.

"Hey!" they called up to the old father on the donkey.
"This donkey is beautiful and the tall boy is handsome.
You just look like an ugly useless old monkey sitting up
there. Why don't you get off and let this handsome boy
ride? The handsome boy riding the pretty donkey will
certainly look splendid together."

Upon hearing the girls' chatter, the son turned to his
father and said, "Papa, now we made a mistake again.
The girls think that you look like a monkey sitting on that
donkey. They say that I should get on the donkey. What
do you think?"

Wearily, his father answered, "First you ride the donkey
and it is a mistake. Then I ride the donkey and it is a
mistake. Now, suppose you come up here and sit in front
of me and we will ride together. How does that sound?"

The boy thought that his father's idea was best, so he
climbed up and sat in front of his father. They continued
on through the village until they reached the custom-
house. The customs officer stopped them and asked,
"Where are you both going with that donkey?"

"Sir," Chow Khok politely answered, "we are taking
the donkey to sell him at the village market on the far
river bank."

The official scowled at him. "That donkey is barely grown," he scolded. "Why are you both sitting on him? You'll break his back and then you'll never be able to sell him. Are you both mad? A little donkey like that! You should carry him."

Chow Khok and his son obediently dismounted and, cradling the donkey in their arms between them, proceeded to walk across the field to the far river bank. A farmer, seeing them walking through the high grass carrying the donkey between them, shouted out, "Hey, you donkey carriers! Our field here is full of sharp thorns. Be careful or the thorns will cut up your legs. Your donkey there is for riding, not carrying. You must be crazy to carry him. Why don't you ride him?"

Chow Khok and his son listened in embarrassment

to the farmer's shouts. Shaking his head hopelessly, Chow Khok complained, "How can we satisfy all the people in this world? When we carried our donkey on a pole, they said we should only carry a pig on a pole. When you rode our donkey, they said that you were an ungrateful son. When I rode our donkey, they said that I looked like a monkey. When we both rode our donkey, they said that we would break his back. Now we carry our donkey in our arms and they say that we are crazy to cut our legs. How can we satisfy all the people in this world? What shall we do now?"

The Cambodian monks constantly reminded the people to use reason and to think for themselves. This story shows what happened to two people who stopped doing so.

APPENDIX
About Cambodia

THAILAND

LAOS

Mekong River

DANGREK MTS.

Angkor

BATTAMBANG

CAMBODIA

② *Tonle Sap*

MOI PLATEAU

③

CARDAMOM MTS.

Tonle Sap River

Mekong River

KRATIEH

ELEPHANT MTS.

① KOMPONG CHAM

Phnom Penh

VIETNAM

GULF OF SIAM

Mekong River

Ho Chi Minh City
(Saigon)

SOUTH CHINA SEA

N

CAMBODIA and
Neighboring Countries

LOCATION OF STORIES:
① Chief Monk of Sohtan Koh
② Chow Prak and Chow Saun
③ The Story of Bhikkhu Sok

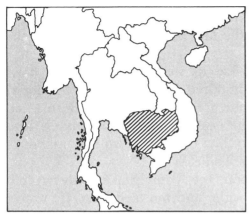

CAMBODIA

Area: 69,898 square miles
Population: 7,200,000
Capital: Phnom Penh

THE LAND

Cambodia is a small country—about the size of the state of Washington, or a little smaller than Great Britain—that is situated toward the southern tip of Southeast Asia. The country is bordered on the north by Thailand and Laos, and on the east by Vietnam, which curves around Cambodia in a sort of crescent-moon shape. To the southwest, the land edges of Cambodia tip into the Gulf of Siam, sprinkling the coastline with small islands. The borders and coastline of the land are lined with mountain ranges and plateaus.

Cambodia is in the tropics, between ten and fifteen degrees north of the equator. Its climate is rather even; the year-round temperature is about eighty degrees Fahrenheit (twenty-seven degrees centigrade) throughout the country. Cambodia has three seasons: a cool season from the end of October to the beginning of March, a hot season from March to the beginning of July, and a rainy season from the middle of July through October. In July, monsoons from the southwestern seas blow across the land, pouring torrents of rain into the rivers and streams, swelling and flooding them. The smaller rivers running together form one of the largest rivers in the world, the Mekong.

The Mekong River has its source in Tibet and flows south for twenty-six hundred miles through the forest gorges of China and Laos, across the borders of Burma and Thailand, and onto the central Cambodian plains. Into the Mekong River also flow the waters from Cambodia's central great lake, the Tonle Sap.

During the dry season, the Tonle Sap is only seventy miles long, two miles wide, and ten feet deep. Its waters flow southward through the Tonle Sap River into the Mekong. In the rainy season, the monsoon rains and melting Tibetan snows swell the Mekong so that its waters back up into the Tonle Sap River, forcing the flow of this river to change its direction. The waters now flow northward into the Tonle Sap, which rises to a depth of forty feet. The area of the lake triples, and its waters pour over onto miles and miles of surrounding marshes, forests, and lowlands. In this manner, the land is made rich with soil and water good for all living things.

There are four types of land in Cambodia: forested mountains, grasslands, lowlands, and seacoast.

About half of the land is tropical mountain forests covered by dense foliage. In the southwest, two ranges, the Elephant Mountains and the Cardamom Mountains, rise like steep cliffs behind the seacoast. To the north, the Dangrek Mountains stretch for about two hundred miles along the Thai border. To the east, forming the border with Vietnam, are the Moi Plateau highlands with their dense jungles. Gold and silver, blue sapphires and red rubies are buried in these mountains. Colorful parrots, cockatoos, and mynah birds sit on the branches of slender silk-cotton trees and stout banyans. Leopards, tigers, sun bears, elephants, monkeys, and tiny deer live in the forests.

The western and northern mountains of Cambodia slope gently down to the grassy foothills and rolling plains of the central part of the country. Orioles, partridges, and quail feed on the nuts of the trees and on the wild cereal grasses of the plains. Rhinoceroses, mongooses, and cobras inhabit these areas.

In the central parts of Cambodia, near the rivers, are lush lowlands. Feathery pepper trees and thick glossy rubber trees grow in the rich soil of the rivers, marshes, and ponds. Cranes, kingfishers, and egrets fly along the rivers' edges where herds of water buffalo roam about. Throughout the lowlands and marshes of Cambodia, there is plenty of food for all the animals. Tree branches drip with clusters of sweet fruit—mango, litchi, durian, banana, and breadfruit.

In the southwestern part of Cambodia, the wooded mountains dip down to the white shores of the Gulf of Siam. Standing stiffly against the sky are palm trees—tall palmyras, shorter coconut palms, and slender betel palms. Plovers and pelicans live along the sandy beaches. Many varieties of fish—mullet, loach, bass—swim in the waters of the Gulf.

Cambodia is a good land with good living things. It is a good land for people. The land has been like this for thousands of years, long before there were any human beings there.

THE PEOPLE AND THEIR HISTORY

Cambodia was the first great civilization and powerful empire of Southeast Asia whose people created beautiful works of art, literature, and music. About one thousand years ago, this ancient empire—the Khmer Empire—

controlled and influenced almost all of Southeast Asia from the Gulf of Siam to the South China Sea. This territory included much of the present-day nations of Burma, Thailand, Malaysia, and the southern part of Vietnam.

The First Khmer Kingdoms: 300 B.C.(?)–A.D. 802

About two thousand years ago, traders from India and Arabia and travelers from China began to write about two Cambodian sister kingdoms. One was in southern Cambodia near the Mekong River delta. The other was about two hundred miles north, on the Mekong River in lands that are now part of Laos.

The southern Khmer kingdom's ideal location, midway between China and India, made it a great trading center for all of Asia. In about 260 B.C., merchants from India began to arrive to trade their goods. They traded their spices, perfumes, jewels, and fine cloth for the gold and ivory of Cambodia.

In about 200 B.C., nomad warrior tribes had cut off China's northern trade routes to India. China found it easier to ship her goods by sea, stopping at the south Khmer seaports. The Chinese exchanged their valued bronze statues, painted porcelain, silks, and jade for the prized products of Cambodia: ivory, peacock feathers, gold, and silver.

A lasting gift of the Khmers to the world was their development of a unique art form. Homes, temples, and warehouses were decorated with beautiful carvings. The pottery and woven fabrics of the Khmers were exquisite. The people were also skilled in working with gold, silver, bronze, ivory, and coral.

Sometime around A.D. 550, the southern Khmer kingdom suffered from a series of disastrous floods and fires. Irrigation canals were ruined and crops failed. There was not enough food. With people suffering from hunger and disease, the southern Khmer kingdom began to fall apart. Many people fled to the safety of the northern Khmer kingdom.

The northern Khmer king, Bavavarman, was the grandson of the last king of the southern Khmer kingdom. He gradually claimed all of the land of the south, and by 650, the two kingdoms were united as one. There were thirty large cities in the country. In each city, beautifully decorated public buildings and temples of brick were built.

By the year 750, however, Cambodia was suffering from petty quarrels among her princes, each prince claiming the right to be king. Soon the country was divided into small rival kingdoms. Raiders from the Indonesian island of Java took advantage of Cambodia's weakness and attacked her coasts repeatedly. During one raid, the Javanese beheaded a Cambodian king and kidnaped a prince. Then they placed their own puppet ruler on the throne.

The kidnaped Cambodian, Prince Jaya, was taken as a hostage to the court of the Javanese king, where he lived for several years. When he returned to his homeland, he was determined to unite Cambodia once again and to throw off the offensive rule of Java. He mobilized a strong army and eventually conquered the invaders. In 802, he was declared King Jayavarman II. The rule of Jayavarman II began a six-hundred-year period of greatness and glory of the Khmer Empire.

The Classical Khmer Period: 802–1219

In celebration of his victories, Jayavarman II built new cities with temples and palaces intricately carved and decorated. Claiming that he was related to the gods,

Jayavarman ruled as the "divine" king for almost fifty years. When he died in 850, the borders of Cambodia were safe, the crops of the land were good, and the buildings of the cities were true works of art. For the next three hundred years, successive Khmer kings continued to rule over a prosperous country. Each king expanded the cities, building temples and palaces, and improved the water system for crop irrigation.

Indravarman I (reigned 877–889) was known as a brilliant scholar and a good king. He built a large artificial reservoir to irrigate the rice fields and grow crops for the people living in the city. Jayavarman V (r. 968–1001) built schools and libraries for the people. His reign was called "the Age of Learning."

Suryavarman I (r. 1002–1050), a great statesman and builder, was known as "King of the Just Laws." His reign was one of Cambodia's greatest periods of art and architecture. He built a second reservoir, five miles long and one mile wide, for the royal capital.

Suryavarman II (r. 1113–1150) was the most powerful king of ancient Cambodia. To his empire he added the conquered lands of Champa (part of present-day Vietnam), Malay, Thailand, and Burma. In the center of this great empire, he built a magnificent temple, Angkor Wat, the largest religious building the world has known.

After Suryavarman's reign, the kingdom of Champa began to grow more powerful. The king of Champa began a long series of successful raids into Cambodia. In 1177, the Chams attacked Angkor and destroyed everything they could. One of the Cambodian princes rallied the army and finally defeated the Chams. In 1181, he was crowned as King Jayavarman VII.

Jayavarman VII, a devout Buddhist, was determined to build a capital city that no invader could ever again

GATE TO
ANGKOR THOM

destroy. His new city, Angkor Thom, was surrounded by thick walls. In the center of the city, he built his own temple, the Bayon. The Bayon had fifty-four stone towers with huge faces of Jayavarman carved into each of the four sides of each tower.

Unfortunately, as Jayavarman grew older, he became obsessed with the idea that he must build more and more temples to Buddha in gratitude for his good fortune. Jayavarman soon turned the country into a forest of temples and monuments. The great demands he placed upon his people for labor and taxes to build these temples were a crushing burden. Fields were not planted and the irrigation systems were not repaired. Jayavarman VII achieved many things, but after his death in 1219, the people were exhausted and the empire began to fall apart.

The Weakening of Cambodia: 1219–1864

The well-being of Cambodia, like all countries in the southern Asian monsoon regions, depended upon the control of the flooding waters of the rainy season to nourish growing crops. For centuries, each Cambodian king at the beginning of his reign took an oath to protect and care for the canals that guided the flooding river waters gently into the rice fields. But for almost three hundred years, there had been a succession of kings who neglected the waterways and the welfare of the people. The only concern of these kings had been in wasteful wars of aggression and in glory. When the water canals crumbled from disrepair, food harvests were poor.

Soon after the death of Jayavarman VII, crops failed, and people were starving. In search of food and vengeance, many people left their homes in the cities and villages to roam the countryside in angry mobs. Soon, lawlessness, crime, and terror spread throughout the country.

During the 1200s, the Thai nation had become powerful, and its armies had begun raiding the Cambodian border. Until the middle of the 1400s, successive Cambodian kings repulsed the Thai invasions. But with each invasion, Cambodia grew weaker. Finally, in 1444, the Cambodian king gave up Angkor as the capital city. Thailand remained the enemy of Cambodia and continued to raid and plunder the country. From time to time Cambodian kings ceded border lands to Thai kings to maintain the peace.

In 1618, the Cambodian king Chey Chetta asked Vietnam to help him defeat the Thai. The Vietnamese agreed to protect Cambodia in return for the right to begin settlements there. The first Vietnamese settlement on Cambodian soil was the city of Saigon.

During the next thirty years, more and more Vietnamese came to settle along the southeastern coast of Cambodia.

Each time problems arose with Thailand or within the royal families, Vietnam helped. And each time, the price of their help was more Cambodian land. By 1698, Vietnam owned most of the lands of southeastern Cambodia, and by 1800, Cambodia was reduced to half of its size of 1444.

Finally, in 1845, Vietnam and Thailand agreed to a truce. The two nations signed a treaty giving each other the eastern and western parts of Cambodia, respectively, and placing the central part of Cambodia under their joint "protection." They also permitted Prince Ang Duong of Cambodia to be crowned as king, as long as he accepted the treaties and control of Vietnam and Thailand.

Fearful that Cambodia would disappear as a nation, King Ang Duong asked the French to help him regain Cambodia from Vietnam and Thailand. In 1863, Norodom, son of Ang Duong, signed a treaty with France. France would protect Cambodia in return for French trading, military, and political privileges in Cambodia.

The French Protectorate: 1864–1954

In 1864, the "French Protectorate of Cambodia" was announced. Prince Norodom was then crowned as king by representatives of both France and Thailand. During the coronation ceremony, his crown was handed to him by the new French Consul as a reminder of France's authority over the throne of Cambodia.

For several centuries, Cambodia had learned to submit to foreign control, and the country now adjusted to French rule. First, France and Thailand signed a treaty under which the king of Thailand gave up any right to collect taxes from Cambodia. France also promised to protect Cambodia from becoming part of the Vietnamese nation.

In 1884, the French forced King Norodom to sign a new treaty giving France full and complete control of all the affairs of the country. The French consul became the actual ruler of Cambodia with the king existing merely as a symbol of the country and the religion. In 1887, Cambodia became a part of a territory that the French called "French Indochina." This included all of present-day Vietnam, Laos, and Cambodia. After this treaty, the French set up a strong central government under the control of the French consul in Phnom Penh, taking away most of the authority of local Cambodian leaders. From this time on, the Cambodian king was obligated to accept the "advice" of the French in both foreign and domestic affairs. The French control of Cambodia lasted for almost one hundred years.

During World War II, after much of France fell to the Nazis in 1940, the Japanese gained control of French Indochina. The Japanese government encouraged Laos, Vietnam, and Cambodia to declare their independence from France.

At the end of World War II, when Japan was defeated (1945), French troops once more landed in Saigon. The French governor-general requested that Cambodia send a delegation to sign a new treaty for French control of Indochina. King Norodom Sihanouk agreed to send this delegation provided that it would be considered as a "delegation from an independent country." In 1946, the French signed an amended treaty which recognized Cambodia as an independent state. But this "State of Cambodia" was still within the French Union. The French gave Cambodia the right to govern itself, but only with the approval of France.

This 1946 agreement did not really grant Cambodia freedom from French control. Many educated Cambodians were outraged not only with the continuing of French domination but also with King Sihanouk's submission to

France. In 1951, King Sihanouk promised his people that within three years he would get France to grant complete independence to Cambodia.

King Sihanouk then left on a European tour, his "Crusade for Independence." In Europe, he spoke to national leaders about France's oppression, Cambodia's neutrality, and the need for economic assistance to rebuild the country. Next, Sihanouk visited with leaders in Tokyo and Bangkok. In Bangkok, King Sihanouk announced that he would not return to Cambodia until France gave Cambodia complete independence.

In 1953, France finally gave in to international pressures and relinquished its control. Cambodia was now recognized as an independent nation, free to elect its own congress without French approval, free to make its own economic and foreign policy, and free to control its police and courts of law. King Sihanouk returned triumphant to Phnom Penh as the liberator of his country.

Independence: 1954–

In 1954, at the International Geneva Conference on Indochina, France and Vietnam signed agreements to withdraw all of their armed forces from Cambodia. Cambodia was now a free and independent country, but there still were many problems. Border disputes with Thailand and Vietnam had to be settled. Economic aid was needed from wealthier countries to help Cambodia repair war-damaged roads, schools, industrial plants, and irrigation systems. Training programs were needed to educate the people in the techniques of managing banks, businesses, and factories.

After 1960, the war between North Vietnam (assisted by the Soviet Union) and South Vietnam (assisted by the United States) caused more problems for newly independent Cambodia. Soviet-supported Vietminh guerrillas poured into Cambodia from Vietnam and established bases from which they fought American and South Vietnamese troops. War was again on Cambodian soil.

A group of Cambodians who were displeased with Sihanouk's policies rebelled. Sihanouk claimed that they were communist allies of the Soviets and Vietminh, and called them the "Khmer Rouge," or Red Khmer. Under their leader, Pol Pot, many of the Khmer Rouge left the cities and set up camps in the northern and western mountains of Cambodia.

Another faction of Cambodians disagreed with Sihanouk's policies and particularly his speeches against the American troops stationed in Vietnam. In 1970, there was an army revolt. Sihanouk was deposed and General Lon Nol installed as chief of state. Lon Nol immediately allied himself with the United States. With an ally now in control of Cambodian policies, the United States helped Cambodia, sending food and money. Unfortunately, because the country was still in disorder, much of this aid found its way into hands of corrupt individuals instead of to the masses of people who needed it.

The Khmer Rouge were still encamped in the countryside, sheltered by the villagers who were anxious for any protection against border raiders. Some of these countryside hamlets also protected the Vietminh. In 1971, with the approval of Lon Nol, the United States Air force began to bomb these "pockets of resistance," and twenty thousand American troops invaded Cambodia. The country became a virtual battleground. By 1973, one-quarter of a million tons of American bombs had been dropped on Cambodia. In August, 1973, the United States Congress voted to stop the bombing.

With the bombing halted, the Khmer Rouge under Pol Pot's leadership began firing rockets into the city of Phnom Penh. Within a few months, the Khmer Rouge was able to enter Phnom Penh victoriously. Then began the time of *peal chur chat,* the "sour and bitter time."

To Pol Pot's thinking, all the tragedies and sufferings of Cambodia were the result of foreign interference— foreign people, foreign ideas, and foreign technology. Pol Pot was convinced that the olden times of Angkor had been a glorious utopia for Cambodia. He was certain that if the people would abandon foreign tools and ideas and once more return to simple rice farming, everyone would be happy and the country would prosper.

Completely convinced of the evils of Western ways, Pol Pot devised a plan of action. He ordered his Khmer Rouge army to evacuate the entire population of the city of Phnom Penh—two million people—and force them into the countryside. At gun point, often with brute force, the citizens of Phnom Penh were driven from their homes. The city was soon depopulated. With the capital now virtually empty, Pol Pot ordered his men to destroy every-thing in the city that was foreign—money, television sets, refrigerators, air conditioners, washing machines, and the like. All schools were shut down. Many libraries and museums were burned.

Most of the exiled inhabitants now swarmed along country roads in the dazed, chaotic manner of displaced refugees. Families were separated. Some were sent to live in barracks. Some worked as prisoners in the rice fields. Anyone who was suspected of previously working for foreigners was executed. Any person heard speaking a foreign language or suspected of having a foreign education was killed. Many were simply thrown into mass graves. From 1975 to 1979, through overwork, starvation, torture and execution, it is estimated that three million of a total population of seven million Cambodians died.

In 1976, fearing a border expansion by Vietnam, Pol Pot's armies began a vicious campaign to rid Cambodia of all Vietnamese living within the country. Many of the Vietnamese had been living in Cambodia for generations. Pol Pot ordered his guerrillas to search out all Vietnamese living in the cities and villages and to kill them. Then the Khmer Rouge began attacks across the border into Vietnam itself. The outraged Vietnamese struck back. In 1978, they invaded Cambodia.

In response, Pol Pot ordered his guerrillas to burn the land and to destroy the crops so that the advancing Vietnamese army would have no food. This "scorched earth" policy resulted in a terrible famine throughout Cambodia. Millions of people died from hunger.

With the country in chaos, the earth scorched, and the people sick and starving, the Vietnamese armies easily captured Phnom Penh and installed their own government. They appointed Heng Samrin as president. Since 1979, two hundred thousand Vietnamese troops have been stationed in Cambodia. And Cambodia, as so many times before in her history, is ruled again by a foreign power—this time the Vietnamese.

Since 1975, Cambodian refugees have fled from American bombings, Pol Pot, and the Vietnamese to the borders of Thailand for protection. In these border camps, homeless refugees wait for international relief organizations to give them the opportunity to begin a new life. Almost four hundred thousand of these political refugees have now been resettled in foreign countries.

Today, descendents of the ancient Khmer people are living in three places: Cambodia, Thai border refugee camps, and in foreign nations as political refugees. The

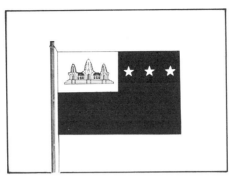

NATIONAL FLAG

people remaining in Cambodia are trying to piece together their lives and traditions under Vietnamese rule; the people in refugee camps await repatriation to friendly nations where they can try to rebuild their lives; the refugees in foreign nations are trying both to keep their ancient traditions and to learn the cultural traditions of their newly adopted nations.

These people, remnants of a once rich and powerful society, have lived through the total and violent collapse of their country. From day to day, they wait for wars and violence to end, as they have so many times in centuries past.

Cambodians have a way of saying good-bye: "May you meet only good and overcome all your enemies."

May the Cambodians, wherever they live, meet only good, and may the enemies of Cambodia not overcome them.

VILLAGE LIFE AND CELEBRATIONS

From time immemorial, the heart and soul of Cambodia has been the village. Kings and invaders would come and go, but the village was always there. Along the rivers which eternally flowed out to the sea, the Cambodians built their homes and temples with a certain confidence that the rhythm of the river would provide a continuing peace and harmony.

During the rainy season, when the monsoon winds brought the rains that flooded over the river banks, the fields were plowed for the planting of rice. Humped gray-blue water buffaloes pulled the farmers' wooden plows across the land, patiently hollowing one deep furrow after another. The river waters flowed into the furrows in endless shining ribbons.

Each family—mother, father, and children—worked together to push the rice seedlings deep into the rich soil of the watered furrows. It was hard work, but everything that was planted grew with an orderly sureness. Soon, the brown bamboo homes of the village were surrounded by fields of rice, vegetables, and fruit in various shades of green, yellow, and orange.

Each day long before dawn, the people of the village began to gather their goods for the marketplace. They filled baskets with produce—cabbages, mangoes, papayas —and pork, chicken, and shrimp. Balancing the baskets gracefully on their heads, the villagers carried them to the market square. Some of the people arranged their wares on bamboo mats; others sat in shaded stalls. Always, the market square was a lively center of village life—selling, buying, and bargaining; talking, laughing, and eating. But before midday, marketing was over, and the people had left the village square to return to work in their homes and fields.

Sometimes, when work was over and the sun had set, the people drifted back to the market square. The men and boys brought out their bamboo drums, long-necked violins, and decorated xylophones. Everyone joined in the singing of familiar songs. Young people danced the graceful Cambodian *lamthon*. Storytellers told again the well-loved folktales. And always, the families were together. Mother, father, and children sitting together, singing together, and listening together.

Because good farmland was always plentiful in Cambodia, there never was a wealthy class of landlords who owned any especially rich land. Instead, the land belonged to any family that worked on it. In each village, each family owned enough land to produce enough food to feed the family. In this manner, each family was independent, living with dignity, and not subservient to any greedy landlord.

Every member of the family was equally important, husband and wife, son and daughter. Each newborn child was given a special single name chosen by the parents and astrologers. This single name possessed a great deal of

MUSICAL INSTRUMENTS

personal meaning for the future life and happiness of the child.

The wife was responsible for the education of the children and the running of the household. She was the family treasurer, planning the selling of family wares and the buying of needed supplies. Girls learned about household affairs from their mothers. Parents hoped that their daughters would bring honor to the family by choosing a husband of good character.

The husband was responsible for the most demanding physical work and for training his sons in farming. Before getting married, every young man was expected to honor the village by becoming a Buddhist monk for one year. Living in the village temple, or *wat*, the young men helped the monks with religious ceremonies and festivals, and learned the treasured teachings of the Buddha.

In the center of every village, the Cambodians built a winged-roofed temple to honor the Buddha, who had shown them the right way to live. Inside the *wat* were statues of Buddha and pictures about his life. The villagers would bring fresh flowers, fruit, and sweet-smelling incense candles to place around the statues in appreciation of Buddha's teachings. To the villagers, the *wat* was not only a place of comfort and quiet meditation, but also a center for their ceremonies and festivals. There, Buddhist monks helped the people to understand their problems and to lead a better life. The monks were teachers, counselors, healers, and community leaders.

Wedding Ceremony

A wedding is one of the most joyous of all Cambodian celebrations. The pre-nuptial rituals and the marriage ceremony are based upon very ancient traditions.

Appointed representatives of the prospective bride and

groom visit with the families and indirectly begin to talk about the possibility of marriage. As the families reach agreement, gifts of special plants and food are brought to the bride's family by the matchmakers. Upon reaching final agreement, the families consult an astrologer to decide upon a favorable date for the wedding.

The wedding ceremony is performed at the bride's house, in keeping with the ancient Cambodian tradition of paying honor to the woman as the administrator of the household affairs. For the wedding day, special foods are made in the form of cylindrical cakes filled with sticky rice or sweet coconut. Silver platters of fruit and meat are laid out in rows on mats around which the guests sit and visit. Musicians entertain the guests, playing traditional songs on their ancient instruments.

During the first part of the wedding, three chosen good women guide the bride and three chosen good men guide the groom into the ceremony room. The bride and groom exchange gifts and rings. The men and women question the bride and groom about their past behavior and their thoughts for living a good life. The wedding guests prod the bride and groom with advice, gentle jokes, and soft laughter. Always, the atmosphere is filled with feelings of kindly affection and harmony. Then the bride and groom are guided out of the ceremony room to await the second part of the wedding ritual.

The guests visit, the musicians play, and after a while, the bride and groom are led back to the ceremony room for the ritual of the Cutting of Hair.

A dancer is selected as the barber. Chanting, he begins to dance around the bride and groom. With a pair of scissors and a comb in his hands, he pretends to cut small pieces of hair from the heads of the couple and puts the "hair" into a bowl of banana leaves. Then each guest in turn symbolically cuts hairs from the bride and groom, and sprinkles the couple with perfume while whispering good wishes to them. The bowl of banana leaves with the hair cuttings are then placed ouside the house as a ritual to remove all bad luck from the life of the couple.

After this ceremony, the guests all feast, and everyone enjoys each other's company.

Important Cambodian Holidays

• THE NEW YEAR: April 13–15. This festival is a beautiful holiday that takes place at the beginning of the planting season. For three days, the people of the village celebrate by visiting each other, bringing special foods to the *wat*, and enjoying age-old music and dances.

The New Year is the time that the young village girls, trained since they were eight years old, perform the classical Cambodian dances. As they dance with their golden gowns and their graceful fingers and hands, the girls look like the exquisite *apsara* (heavenly dancers) carved on the walls of the ancient Cambodian temples more than a thousand years ago.

Each New Year, the Cambodian villagers are once again enchanted by their delicate dancers. And, once again, they listen reverently to the yellow-robed monks chanting the prayers of Buddha. They are grateful for the returning rains of the rice season. They are at one again with their ancient heritage.

• PLANTING OF THE HOLY FURROW: May 10–12. This ceremony marks the beginning of work in the rice fields. To signify this, the king plowed a furrow and the queen sowed seeds behind the plow. Then, different kinds of food such as rice and corn were put in a silver tray for the royal oxen to eat. If the oxen chose to eat the rice first, the people

believed that the rice crop would be good that year; if the oxen chose to eat the corn first, then the corn crop would be good.

• BUDDHA ENTERS NIRVANA: May 15. This holiday observes the triple events of Buddha's birth, his enlightenment, and his death, at which time he entered nirvana. The Cambodian people go to the *wat,* bringing food to the monks and offering incense and flowers as they ask for the blessing of Buddha.

• RETREAT OF THE MONKS: July–October. This ceremony lasts three months, during which the monks must not travel and must always stay in the *wat,* studying and meditating to gain merit. Special handmade candles burn day and night for the entire period. Many young boys enter the monkhood during this time. In doing so, they show respect to Buddha and gratitude to their parents.

• THE CEREMONY OF THE ANCESTORS: September. The spirits of dead people are remembered during this time. Children, in order that they may have a better life, offer food to Buddha to release any ancestral sins. Each family takes turns bringing offerings to the *wat*. The monks recite stories and give talks to the families on how to make a better life for themselves.

• THE WATER FESTIVAL: November 10–12. This is a happy holiday started by kings of bygone centuries. It is a time when the Mekong River is at its highest from the monsoon rains. According to legend, the festival pleases the god of the river, who will make the rice crop good and the country prosperous. For three nights, decorated illuminated boats sail up the river. People from the cities and villages gather at the riverbank to watch boats, sing, dance, and feast.

GLOSSARY

Angkor: an ancient Khmer word that originally meant "organiza-
   tion" and later "city." The great capital city of the Khmer
   Empire was called Angkor.

angsakh: an apron made of silk; one of the three items of a monk's set
   of clothing

apsara: a heavenly female dancer written about in Cambodian literature and beautifully depicted in Khmer sculpture and paintings

baht: Thai currency

bhikkhu: a Buddhist monk

Bodhisattva: a divine human being who could enter nirvana and
   experience the ultimate perfect happiness, but who refuses to
   do so in order to devote himself to helping others in this world.
   This concept of Buddhism appealed to many Buddhist kings, who
   called themselves Bodhisattvas and convinced the people that
   they were gods on earth who were to be worshiped.

Brahman: a member of the highest caste in India

Brahmani: a female member of the Brahman caste

Buddha: literally, "awakened one," "enlightened one"; derived from
   budh, "to awake"; someone who has become enlightened by the
   highest possible understanding and knowledge. "Buddha" is
   really a title, not the name of a person. Gautama Siddhartha, the
   historical founder of Buddhism who lived in India about 500
   B.C., is often called "Buddha" or "the Buddha."

Buddhism: the name given to the teachings of Gautama Siddhartha, the Buddha. Buddhism is not a religion in the Western sense, but is a moral and ethical way of life. It emphasizes honesty and compassion and rejects the concept of gods and saints. All men and women are considered equal, and there is no caste system or aristocracy.

There are two main branches of Buddhism: Theravada (literally, the ancients' wisdom), the older branch, practiced by the people of Cambodia, Burma, Laos, Sri Lanka, and Thailand; and Mahayana (literally, great vehicle), practiced by people in Japan, China, and other countries. Mahayana Buddhists call the Theravada branch Hinayana, or "small vehicle."

buffalo boy: a young boy who takes care of grazing buffaloes

Cambodia: the English form of "Cambodge," the French word for the nation

caste: a system of social status based upon heredity used by the Hindus of India. A caste is a closed group whose members are severely restricted in their choice of marriage partners, occupation, and place of residence. In India, there were five castes: (1) the Brahmans, priests and scholars; (2) the Kshatriyas, warriors and rulers; (3) the Vaisyas, farmers and merchants; (4) the Sundras, peasants and laborers; and (5) the Panchamas, untouchables who perform the most menial tasks.

cheyporh: a monk's outer robe; one of the three items of a monk's set of clothing

Chow: a grandson, a young boy; a term added to a personal name and used by older people when addressing a boy. It can sometimes be used with a man's name to imply that the man is a simpleton.

gati: literally, "the way"; the right moral and ethical way in which people should live

Gatiloke: the name of the large body of Cambodian Buddhist folk stories that was gathered over the centuries. The word "Gatiloke" means something like "the right way to live for the people of the world." When these stories were written down at the end of the nineteenth century, the collection was given the title *Gatiloke.*

Himalaya Mountains: a mountain range in south-central Asia. The highest peak in the world, Mount Everest, is one of the Himalayas. Hindus believe that these mountains are the home of their gods.

Hinduism: a religious and social system that grew up in India about four thousand years ago

Indochina: a term applied by the French to their former colonies—Laos, Cambodia, and Vietnam. The word "Indochina" is also used as a geographical term for the large peninsula including these countries, but it is often offensive to the peoples of them. There is no such thing as an "Indochinese" people or language. The peoples of "Indochina" are as different from each other as the peoples of Europe are.

Ishvara: the Lord; the Highest Self; the Absolute Power; a Hindu concept of God

Iso: the Cambodian name for the Hindu god Siva. Siva, often depicted riding a bull, is associated with both destruction and peace.

Jaya: a Cambodian name meaning "victory," "victorious." It was often used by princes and kings of Cambodia (for example, Jayavarman).

Kampuchea: the Cambodian word for Cambodia. The word "Kampuchea" is derived from "Kambuja," the name of a legendary hero who arrived from the west, married a princess of the land, and founded the Cambodian nation. "Kampuchea" implies "children of Kambuja."

khak: a Cambodian coin of small denomination

Khmer: The name that the people of Cambodia sometimes call themselves and their language. "Khmer" means "the children of Mera." Mera was the legendary mother of the Cambodians.

Khmer Empire: the great Cambodian civilization that lasted from A.D. 802 to 1219.

koh: island

kruu: teacher; also used with a teacher's name as his title

lamthon: a slow, graceful Cambodian dance

lay devotee: a person who believes in a religion and who supports monasteries and monks with gifts, but who does not himself become a monk

loke: the world

mantra: an incantation, spell, charm, or hymn; used in the ceremonies of Hindus and of some Buddhist sects

Moslem: a member of a religious group comprising the majority of the people living in the western parts of Asia, the Malay Peninsula, and Indonesia. Their religion is called Islam. Moslems are a minority group in Cambodia and are often the victims of prejudice.

nirvana: in Buddhism, a state of supreme bliss and liberation for a human being; the end of the pain of suffering and desires. Nirvana can be achieved after numerous deaths and rebirths.

novice: a person studying to be a monk

Pandide: a Sanskrit word meaning "scholar"

Phnong: the name given to tribes of people who live in the mountains of Cambodia. The word *phnong* means "savage" in Cambodian.

praek: the horizontal outer wooden frame around the wheel of a Cambodian oxcart

reincarnation: the belief that the soul of a person who dies is "transferred" to the body of another. Sometimes this is called "transmigration of the soul" or "rebirth." The belief came about as primitive peoples noticed the cycles of birth and death and saw that children resembled their parents. As a religious doctrine, reincarnation appeared in India in about 600 B.C. and was later adopted into Buddhism.

riel: Cambodian money of relatively large denomination

Sanskrit: literally, "perfected"; the most ancient language of the scriptures of Hinduism. Sanskrit became a formal court language and was used in this manner by Cambodian kings who identified themselves with Hindu gods. Like Latin, Sanskrit is no longer used except by some scholars and religious groups.

slathorbysay: a Buddhist ceremonial prayer altar arranged with incense, flowers, fruit, and candles. It is made of a *bysay,* which is a section of a banana-tree trunk to which layers of banana leaves rolled up in finger-shapes are attached.

sen: Cambodian money of small denomination; worth about a penny

Southeast Asia: the large peninsula that includes the countries of Burma, Thailand, Laos, Vietnam, and Cambodia. The term is sometimes used to include other countries of the region, such as Malaysia, the Philippines, and Indonesia.

spong: a loincloth; one of the three items of a monk's set of clothing

sraa: a Cambodian alcoholic drink made by fermenting rice

Surya: an ancient Cambodian word meaning "sun." It was often used in the names of Cambodian rulers (for example, Suryavarman).

Tah: a grandfather, an old man; a term added to a personal name and used by a younger person when addressing an older man. It is sometimes added to a man's name to denote laziness or ineptness.

Taxila: a city that was a center of learning in about 300 B.C. Its site is in present-day Pakistan.

tbal kdoong: a rice mill with a large foot-powered pestle (grinder) made of wood and a hard stone plate underneath used as a mortar. Rice is placed on the stone plate. A person jumping up and down on a wooden lever attached to the pestle can grind the rice into a fine powder.

Ten Precepts: a set of rules for conduct that Buddhist monks must follow. The Ten Precepts are almsgiving, morality, self-denial, wisdom, fortitude, patience, truth, determination, goodwill, and neutrality.

Theravada: *see* Buddhism

Varman: a Cambodian word meaning "protector." It was added to the names of Cambodian princes when they became king (for example, Jayavarman, Indravarman).

Veda: literally, "knowledge"; the religious scriptures of the Hindus. The most important Vedas are the Rig-Veda (old Veda), the Sama-Veda (chants), and the Yajur-Veda (sacrificial prayers).

wat: the central hall of worship (temple) in a Buddhist monastery

RECOMMENDED READING

Briggs, Lawrence P. *The Ancient Khmer Empire*. Philadelphia: American Philosophical Society, 1951.

> Perhaps the most detailed source book and bibliography on the history, art, and architecture of Cambodia from A.D. 100 to 1500. The book also contains an excellent discussion of biased translations and conflicting interpretations of Cambodian history by the Chinese, Thai, and French. Illustrated.

Cady, John F. *Thailand, Burma, Laos and Cambodia*. Englewood Cliffs, N.J.: Prentice-Hall, 1966.

> A good historical perspective on the interrelationships of these Theravada Buddhist nations of Southeast Asia.

Coedes, Georges. *The Making of Southeast Asia*. Berkeley: University of California Press, 1966.

> A description of the political and cultural development of the Southeast Asian peninsula by the famous French scholar who devoted his life to the study of that region. Most Cambodian histories are based upon Coedes' translations of the ancient Khmer stone inscriptions.

Edmonson, Monro S. *Lore*. New York: Holt, Rinehart and Winston, 1971.

> A good, readable perspective of the cultural meaning of folklore, showing similarities of themes and types of stories throughout the world. Historical charts of known written world literature from 3500 B.C. to the present are included in the book.

Groslier, Bernard-Philippe. *The Arts and Civilization of Angkor*. New York: Frederick A. Praeger, 1957.

> Detailed analysis and commentary on Cambodian art by the eminent French scholar who devoted years to unraveling the history of the Khmer Empire and to restoring the ancient buildings of Angkor.

Hall, D.G.E. *A History of Southeast Asia*. 4th ed. New York: St. Martin's Press, 1981.

> The most detailed book in English on the history of Cambodia from neolithic times to the present. There are excellent introductory comments on the problems of biased historical reports by ancient Chinese chroniclers, Thai translations, and modern European colonial powers.

Harrison, Brian. *Southeast Asia: A Short History*. 3rd ed. New York: St. Martin's Press, 1967.

> A good short history of Southeast Asia, more readable than Hall's work.

Huffman, Franklin E. *English-Khmer Dictionary*. New Haven: Yale University Press, 1978.

Jenner, Philip, trans. "Tales of Judge Hare." Manoa, Hawaii: Department of Indo-Pacific Languages, University of Hawaii at Manoa. Typescript.

> This is an unpublished translation of a series of popular Cambodian stories about a clever rabbit. A copy of the translation may be obtained from the University of Hawaii at Manoa.

National Geographic. April, 1960; October, 1964; March, 1971; May, 1982.

> Major portions of these issues are devoted to the ancient and modern history of Cambodia. There are excellent photographs and artistic renditions that recreate the daily life of the ancient Khmer Empire.

Rahula, Walpola. *What the Buddha Taught*. Bedford, England: The Gordon Frazer Gallery, 1959.

> A very readable book on the concepts and values of Buddhism from the Theravada Buddhist point of view. (Most of the materials on Buddhism in the English language present a Mahayana interpretation.)

Rawson, Philip. *The Art of Southeast Asia*. New York: Frederick A. Praeger, 1947.

> An excellent, readable book with photos of Southeast Asian art objects and architecture dated from 500 B.C. to A.D. 1500.

Schecter, Jerrold. *The New Face of Buddha: Buddhism and Political Power in Southeast Asia.* New York: Coward-McCann, 1967.

> A good analysis of traditional values and changing perspectives of religion in Southeast Asia.

Seal, Betty, ed. "Cambodian Legends, Proverbs, History." Long Beach, Calif.: Long Beach Unified School District, 1978. Typescript.

> Papers collected by the school district's Director of Indochinese Projects. (Long Beach has one of the largest Cambodian refugee populations in the United States.)

Steinberg, David. *Cambodia: Its People, Its Culture.* New Haven: Human Relations Area File Press, 1959.

> The most informative book on Cambodia, including discussions of traditional culture, political history, education, economy, and government. The book is very well written and is probably the most respectable and unbiased resource available.